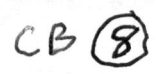

# MURDER AND DECEPTION

A HOPE HERRING COZY MYSTERY BOOK 8

J. A. WHITING

NELL MCCARTHY

Copyright 2022 J.A. Whiting and Whitemark Publishing

Cover copyright 2022 San Coils: www.coverkicks.com

Formatting by Signifer Book Design

Proofreading by Donna Rich: donnarich@me.com

This book is a work of fiction. Names, characters, places, or incidents are products of the author's imagination or are used fictitiously. Any resemblance to locales, actual events, or persons, living or dead, is entirely coincidental.

All rights reserved.

No part of this publication can be reproduced or transmitted in any form or by any means, electronic or mechanical, without permission in writing from J. A. Whiting.

**To hear about new books and book sales, please sign up for my mailing list at:**
**www.jawhiting.com**

❈ Created with Vellum

*With thanks to our readers*

*Dream big*

# 1

Hope leaned back in her chair and stared at the computer screen. She had read many of her husband's short essays, and while some of them were painful, none were as dour and dark as the one she had just finished. She wished her husband was around to explain the essay. She wished he could tell her it was an exercise in sci-fi experimentation. It was nothing more than the start of a story, a story set in some sort of dystopian nightmare.

But her husband had never written fiction, especially, not science fiction. He had been a journalist, a reporter who chased interviews with prominent people, politicians, captains of industry, billionaires. It wasn't that her husband didn't like fiction, didn't read fiction. It was just that he didn't write it. He always told her that the truth was stranger than fiction to begin with.

He chased stories that most writers couldn't imagine on their best, drug-induced nights. They couldn't dream what he investigated. He saw far worse and far better than those novelists who wore the blinders of living inside their heads. Hope believed him. He focused on people, and people could be unpredictable.

She would have liked to ask her husband about the essay, but that was impossible. Her husband was dead, the victim of a one-car accident on a dry, straight road, under a bright sun and a cloudless sky. She had always wondered about the accident. She had never really believed the official explanation, but she had no way to investigate. She had accepted and moved from Ohio to North Carolina. She had taken her daughter with her. She had fled. She thought it would be easier, and it would have been, if she hadn't read the ... essay.

"Good evening, Mrs. Herring."

Hope turned to the voice. "Hello, Max."

Max stood a few feet away wearing the black suit he had been wearing since he was buried almost a century before. The ghost, with his serious look and voice, had come with the house. He'd also come with a mystery. A hundred years ago, Max had been murdered, and he would not rest or cross to the other side until he solved the crime. He needed to know. It was that simple and that difficult. He needed to know who killed him.

And a few months ago, he and Hope had figured it out. But Max didn't leave ... he didn't cross over. He decided he wanted to stay in the house a little longer with Hope and her young teenaged daughter Cori.

"Mrs. Herring, how are you this evening?"

"I'm quite well, and you?"

"As you are aware, my condition does not change. Well, my physical condition is set in stone, so to speak. However, my mental state changes all the time."

"You're happy to have solved your murder, though."

"I am. While many clues pointed in a certain direction, we were able to sort it out and discover the identity of my killer. My goal was reached." The ghost straightened up. "And now it is my turn to help you. I will do research to figure out what happened to your dear husband."

"I don't know if that's a good idea, Max. It could prove to be a dangerous thing to do."

"Mrs. Herring. What danger could befall me? I am already dead."

"But ... investigating could bring danger to Cori."

"And to you?"

"Yes, to me, as well." Hope breathed deeply. "But I'll allow you to dive deep into his history and see what you can find. We'll decide later what to do with any information you might discover."

"You are most kind, Mrs. Herring. I do love to use your computer to facilitate my searching. There seems to be no end to the information and knowledge reachable by computer. I am quite amazed."

"We all are, Max. Don't worry about reaching any sort of end. You can spend the rest of your life ... well, your after-life searching the net. It's both a boon and a curse."

"I shall remember that. It's that time of year again, isn't it?"

"What time is that?" Hope pushed a strand of her shoulder-length brown hair from her forehead.

"October, Halloween. Cori is planning on a costume, correct?"

"She is, and I have to come up with something, too. There's a school-sponsored party that I'm scheduled to attend. So, I have to dress in costume for the event."

"A masquerade? Oh, I do love masquerades. In my day, they were the most fun of all. My wife and I would spend the evening guessing who was who. Sometimes, the masks were so elaborate that we couldn't figure it out. The music and dancing were top notch, and the galas were always well attended."

"This isn't a real masquerade party, but more of a costume dance. I suppose there will be music, and the theme will be normal Halloween fare. I might just put a sheet over my head and call myself a ghost."

Max chuckled. "I do wonder sometimes how ghosts became sheets. I suppose the ones that rose from the grave would have been wearing a shroud. As you can see, I am wearing what I was buried in."

"And, it's held up quite nicely."

They both laughed.

"I shall leave you to your work," Max said.

"My work is over. It's time for bed. I have school tomorrow, and I'll need to be sharp."

"May I use the computer while you sleep?"

"Of course, but would you close the blinds on the windows? People will think I'm up all night surfing the net."

"Yes, I see. I will make your office as dark as possible."

"No need to exaggerate. There aren't many people who will look at the attic windows to begin with. The ones who might catch a glimpse will probably think I don't use a screensaver."

"Nevertheless, I will do what I can to be discreet. Thank you."

"It's nothing, Max. Have a good night."

"Good night, Mrs. Herring."

Max faded away, and Hope rose, stretching. No matter how many times she told Max to just call her by her first name, the ghost continued to use Mrs. Herring when he addressed her. Hope figured it was probably due to his upbringing.

The weekend had been a busy one. Her muscles ached from her Saturday at the Butter Up Bakery where she worked as a part-time baker once a week. Edsel, the owner, had asked Hope to make as many pumpkin cookies as possible, and while there were machines to knead the dough, the work was repetitive. Her arms felt ready to fall off by the time she was finished. Sunday had provided some recovery, but she needed a good night's sleep.

Hope found Cori in bed, earbuds blocking out all outside sound. Cori's long, brown hair was tied in a ponytail, which made her look older than she was. It wouldn't be too long before Cori was looking at colleges and doing applications, and Hope didn't exactly look forward to that.

Hope taught at the middle school, and the students could be challenging at times. Coming of age was never an easy thing. Many cultures recognized that by inventing special ceremonies for the event.

She touched her daughter on the shoulder and Cori looked up, her blue eyes questioning. Then, she tapped her iPad, ending whatever she was listening to.

"Podcast?" Hope asked.

"Yeah, National Geographic. Did you know that otters hold hands while they sleep, so they don't float away from each other?"

"Is that true? Of course, the question becomes why do they sleep in water."

"That's another podcast, I suppose. I'm pretty sure I don't want to be an otter. Although, floating and swimming might be fun."

"Never mind. Ready for school tomorrow?"

Cori nodded. "Homework's done."

"Then, lights out in five."

Cori frowned. "I have seventeen minutes left on this podcast. Is that all right?"

"Sure, but brush your teeth while you're listening. Seventeen minutes will turn into half an hour if you do things one at a time."

"Roger that."

"Roger that? Since when did you pick up military lingo?"

"Don't know, but all the kids in school use it."

"Oh, have you given any thought to your Halloween costume this year?"

"Witch. I don't think I can go wrong if I'm a witch."

"All right. If you need any help, let me know. Luke's coming over for a cup of tea. We'll sit out on the porch so we don't disturb you."

"Roger that."

Hope laughed and left the room. She knew that "roger that" would become something else in a week or two. Kids changed their language on a regular basis. She couldn't keep up with the slang, and she didn't bother to try. Hope trusted that Cori would revert to the Queen's English at some point, and that would be good enough.

When she got the text from Luke, Hope made tea, put on her jacket, and carried the mugs out to the front porch. She'd been seeing Luke Donlan casually for some time, but the relationship hadn't progressed beyond hand-holding and sweet kisses.

Hope still felt awkward about seeing another man, and they'd both agreed to move slowly.

Luke was just coming up the walkway to the porch when Hope stepped outside to meet him.

"Good timing." Luke hugged her and accepted a mug before they sat down in the porch chairs. Tall and slender with muscular arms and shoulders, the man had sandy-colored hair, dark brown eyes, and a warm and friendly smile. He owned a landscaping business and he'd met Hope when he came to give her an estimate on some yard work. They'd enjoyed each other's company since then, hiking, biking, taking walks, and having dinner together.

"It's a nice night." Hope sipped from her mug. "How was your day?"

"Crazy busy. It's always a mad rush during fall cleanup time. So much has to be done in such little time. And we're finishing up a few landscaping projects. The whole team is working overtime. I'll probably nod off in this rocking chair."

Hope chuckled. "I'll be right here next to you snoring my head off." She told him about her day and what was on tap for the coming week.

"I'll bet Cori and her friends are excited for Halloween." Luke rocked gently back and forth.

"They are. I love Halloween. This year, the

middle school where I work is putting on a costume gala. The staff is encouraged to go so I'll need a costume. Want to come?"

Luke smiled. "I'd love to, but I don't know if I'd be able to stay awake that late."

"Believe me, I understand. If you change your mind, just let me know."

"So what are you going to be for Halloween?"

"Not sure yet. An evil teacher?"

Luke laughed. "I don't think you'd be able to pull that off. You're too nice."

Hope's eyes widened. "Maybe you should talk to my students. You might end up changing your mind about that."

After more chit-chat, Luke asked about her research into her husband's death. "Have you discovered anything new?"

With a sigh, Hope shook her head. "I've been slacking. I know it's awful, but I haven't had the energy to do anything on the case. I feel guilty about it, but the more important thing is that it worries me. The detective back in Ohio warned me off looking into the accident. If someone killed Doug because of what he was investigating, then Cori and I could be in danger if I try to figure out what happened."

Luke was quiet for a few moments. "You could let it go. Leave it alone. Nothing will bring Doug back."

"But I made a promise to myself that I'd find out who hurt him," Hope said quietly.

Luke took Hope's hand in his. "You could do some research. If Doug was killed because he was getting too close to something that someone wanted left alone, I doubt you looking into a few things would trigger them to come after you. You're a teacher, not an investigative journalist. On the other hand, their reaction might depend on what you stumble onto. It's a decision you'll have to make. But give it a lot of thought before picking it up again."

After Luke left and she was getting ready for bed, she pushed the worries of Doug's accident from her mind and turned her thoughts to the next school day. She remembered that in the morning, there would be a moment of silence for Cameron Pender, the student who had died a year ago.

A talented cheerleader, Cameron had suffered a broken neck when a cheer pyramid had collapsed. Hope wasn't familiar with all the details since it happened before she started working at the school, but the injury had led to other medical problems, that led to more problems, that eventually led to the teen's death. Now, the school was going to have a little acknowledgement on the anniversary of Cameron's passing.

For a moment, Hope wondered if Cameron had become a ghost like Max.

After the moment of silence, Hope was going to give her class a quiz. They wouldn't like that, but she had warned them on Friday. Her better students would be prepared. Her not-so-good students would groan and grumble and struggle. There was nothing she could do about that. Poor students were poor students for a reason. It wasn't an act of God. After her years in the classroom, Hope recognized her limitations. She couldn't make an Einstein out of a class clown. That was strictly up to the student. She could influence them only so much.

Hope pushed Doug's accident, the quiz, school, and the moment of silence from her head. She needed to concentrate on a real problem—what was she going to wear to the school Halloween gala?

## 2

October was Hope's favorite month of the year. In Castle Park, North Carolina, the days were still warm, and the nights were mostly cool. The season's overnight temperatures dropped below fifty, which meant the Bermuda grass that everyone cut would stop growing. There was no frost to contend with. If the leaves didn't turn colors right away, as they did in Ohio, that was all right with Hope. She could wait for November, for Thanksgiving. While the days were getting shorter, there was still nearly two months before the shortest day of the year.

"Are we going to the Halloween party at school?" Cori asked from the passenger seat as Hope drove them to school.

"Why do you ask? Don't you want to go?"

"I don't know. There will be a lot of adults there, right?"

"I suppose so. It's for the entire school. Are you thinking you don't want to go?"

"I haven't decided. I mean, Lottie isn't sure she wants to go, and I wouldn't want her to be all alone."

"She has parents. She won't be alone."

"She will be, if they decide to go to the party."

"What I'm hearing is that you're angling to stay home with Lottie, either at her house or ours. Is that right?"

"Well, I'm just trying to help out my friend. You'd do the same for your friend ... if you had one."

"I have plenty of friends, so don't go there, Miss Know-It-All. And, I'm not at all inclined to leave you and Lottie behind."

"Why? It's not like we're bad kids. We never get into trouble. Well, I don't get into trouble."

"Neither does Lottie, not really."

"To tell the truth, Mom, I remember the haunted house from before. I don't want that to happen to me again."

Cori was referring to a haunted house where she had witnessed a murder and become the next target for the killer. That had not been a good Halloween for her.

"This isn't a haunted house," Hope said. "It's in the school gym. Yes, there will be lots of people in costumes, and some will be ghoulish, but you won't be alone. And I'll remind you that there will be punch and cookies ... pumpkin cookies that I made for Edsel."

"That's tempting, it really is. And, I guess I'll just have to talk Lottie into going."

"Tell her there will be a costume contest. She might win."

"She won't win. She's going as a vampire, and vampires never win."

"Why is that?"

"It's a conspiracy. Vampires are too sexy, so the judges don't pick them."

"What? Vampires are sexy? I didn't know that."

"Didn't you see the Twilight films? Those vampires are not the kind that hide in coffins and wear dark capes."

"So, all Lottie has to do is find a cape and some fangs."

"No, she went online and bought a costume. It's Lady Dracula, and it has a short skirt and a flirty cape. I think it's more for adults than kids."

Hope frowned. "Do her parents know she bought this costume?"

"Not yet. But they will. She used her mother's credit card."

"That doesn't sound like a good plan. I'm guessing her mother will want to see the costume Lottie bought."

"Yeah, well, that won't happen, because Lottie is going to change some things. It won't look like the costume she bought."

"I get it. Her mom will think the costume is one thing, but it's really going to be something else. So, when Lottie goes trick-or-treating, the costume will be a surprise."

"That's pretty much it. Lottie thinks she can get away with it because on Halloween it will be too late for her to get another costume."

"Unless she wears it to the school party."

"Roger that."

"I think you should talk to Lottie. She's already made one mistake in buying an inappropriate costume," Hope suggested.

"It's not inappropriate for some people."

"You know what I mean. Her second mistake is lying about the costume. Lying never does any good, because the lie is always found out. Then, it becomes an embarrassment. While Lottie might think her mother will be forced to let her wear the costume on

Halloween, that isn't guaranteed. Her mother might just nix the whole deal and Lottie will have to stay home."

"Why would she do that? It's just a costume for one night."

"It's not the costume, and it's not the money, since Lottie's mom was willing to spend for it. That's what you have to understand. It's the lying and hiding stuff from her parents. Lottie has a lesson to learn, and it's better that she learns it now, when she's young, than later, when it could be more serious."

Cori leveled her eyes at her mother. "I think you're slipping into lecture mode."

"Lecture mode isn't a bad thing. Or, I should say, it's not a bad thing if you're listening. You can learn a lot from your parents and elders. Believe it or not, they were your age once upon a time."

"I know, but they've forgotten most of what it was like. Besides, things have changed. You didn't have all the stuff we have now."

"It's not stuff. Am I not being clear? It's the inner you that's important. Virtue comes from the inside, and virtue works in every era, everywhere it's tried. Same for vice, which is why you choose virtue over vice."

"Roger that."

Hope quit talking as the latest "roger that" signaled that Cori was no longer going to listen. Hope wanted to offer additional advice and counsel, but she knew it would do little good. When kids tuned out, the learning was over. Hope had seen that a thousand times in class. It was as if they turned some sort of switch. She wished she knew where the switch was, so she could turn it back on.

Hope dropped off Cori and then proceeded to the other middle school where she taught. Once in her classroom, she had a few minutes before the students arrived. That was her "me" time. She had already prepared her lesson plans. Since it was October, she was going to teach them about harvesting crops. She knew some of her students understood farming and harvesting, but most of them had no idea how food came from field to shelf. It was magic for many. They went to the grocery store, and the aisles were full. She wanted them to know that food production required coordination and effort, lots of effort.

At her desk, Hope wondered if Lottie was the best friend Cori could have. It seemed Lottie was conniving to wear a risqué outfit, without her mother knowing. Well, waiting to show it to her mother until there was little time to correct the problem. Of course, Lottie's mom might simply add a sheet to the costume and send Lottie out as a ghost. That would be a quick solution, although it wouldn't really solve the problem. Lottie needed to learn the importance of honesty.

Would Cori want to dump her best friend because of Lottie's lying to her folks?

Not a chance.

Hope would need to find a way to get Cori to help her friend. Everyone would win if Cori could convince Lottie to be honest and truthful. Was that possible? Who knew? But Hope believed that almost anything was possible.

As always, Danielle was the first student through the door. She was a small girl with huge glasses and hunched shoulders. She was the ugly duckling that would probably bloom into a swan when high school came around. At the moment, she suffered from a bit of a complex, although she was a straight A student. Hope guessed Danielle was the quiet mouse that listened more than she spoke, a sure recipe for success.

"Good morning, Mrs. Herring." Danielle headed for her desk. At least she didn't sit at the back of the room.

"Good morning, Danielle, good weekend?"

"Yes. Are we still having the quiz today?"

"Did you study?"

"Oh, I studied, but I thought maybe you might change your mind about giving it."

"Nope, we'll have a quiz right after morning announcements."

"And the moment of silence for Cameron."

"That's right. Did you know Cameron?"

"No, she was older than me."

Hope knew that Cameron meant little to Danielle or to anyone else in the class. Cameron was older, and that meant she was an unknown. It was funny how that happened. Kids who might otherwise have mingled often kept to their own age group when separated into grades. That wasn't an entirely bad thing. Bullies came in all ages and genders. An older, bigger bully might ruin things for the younger group. Perhaps, keeping kids within their own age group was a good idea.

As the room filled with students, Hope stopped her musing. She greeted each and every student by name, a practice she had learned early in her career. Almost everyone liked to hear their name used. She also noted their general demeanor. She had heard too many horror stories about a teacher who failed to notice a troubled student who then went off the rails. That sometimes led to tragedy. If Hope spotted a sick student, she ordered the student to the nurse's office. The problem children didn't get better because they heard her lecture, although she wished she possessed such power.

The students chatted quietly until the announcements started. The principal, Mrs. Warren, began with the date and time and proceeded from there, reminding everyone of the upcoming Halloween Gala. The proceeds would be used to buy books for the school library. Hope wondered about the libraries of the future since the internet provided access to more books than the students could read. She guessed that sooner or later the library of yesteryear might be vanquished by modern ways.

The last item on the agenda was the moment of silence. While most of the students had no memory of Cameron, they dutifully bowed their heads. Some whispered prayers. Most took the moment to steal a last look at their phones. While they weren't supposed to access their phones in school, Hope knew that most of them ignored the rule. But, once class began, if she caught a student with a phone out, she would take it. Sometimes, she returned it after class, sometimes she didn't. If she turned it over to the assistant principal, the student would have detention after classes ended.

Rules were rules.

The moment ended. Hope stood and smiled.

"Phones away if you want to keep them. Books put away, too. We have a quiz, as I promised on Friday."

Half the class groaned.

Hope smiled. "I know you would be terribly disappointed if you didn't have the quiz."

"No, we wouldn't," Norris called out.

"Too late, Norris. Don't say another word." She started to pass out the quizzes. "There's a bonus question on the last page so don't miss it. The question is 'who invented the electromagnetic rotary device?'"

# 3

"I don't know."

Hope looked over at Cori, who seemed distracted. They were in the car on the way home after school.

"Of course, you do. Think. I told you about the inventor while I was preparing the quiz."

"I can't remember."

"You're not trying."

"Why do I have to take the same quiz you give your stupid students?"

"They're not stupid, and neither are you. So, answer the question or tell me what's bothering you."

"Nothing is bothering me."

"Cori, let's not pretend we don't live together. You know when I'm having a bad day, and I know when you are. We're a family. We learn about each other. It makes for a better relationship."

"Okay, okay. It was ... Faraday ... Michael Faraday, right?"

"It was. And you still have the opportunity to share what's bothering you."

"Nothing."

"All right then. Don't say later that you weren't offered the chance. I may be your mother, but that doesn't mean I give horrible advice."

Cori said nothing and Hope took that as a sign to remain silent. As soon as they entered the house, Bijou, their big fluffy brown and white cat, met them at the door, and rubbed against their legs, purring.

Cori picked up the cat and kissed her on top of the head. They went to Cori's room while Hope headed for her attic office. The mother and daughter were like a married couple who were having a disagreement, giving each other the silent treatment. Hope was pretty sure Cori wouldn't be silent for long.

Once in her office, the first thing Hope did was check her email. She wasn't a big fan of email. It was convenient and fast, but it lacked the personal touch of a handwritten letter, which had gone out of style a long time ago. She knew people who did everything online, from evites to e-thankyous. Capital letters were rare, and emojis danced across the screen. The little faces were supposed to sum up someone's feelings. Hope often found them annoying.

She answered the emails that needed answering and thought about unlocking another of her husband's files. He'd left behind a laptop filled with files that were password protected. The passwords were the names of Roman and Greek gods, names he had incorporated into the worst screenplay she had ever encountered. It was a terrible story with terrible dialogue, but it contained the keys to the files.

And, the files contained the last story Doug had investigated. It wasn't a good or uplifting story. It was more of a giant conspiracy to do something about the world's population.

She wasn't in the mood for more dire stories, not after Cori's little snit.

"Good evening, Mrs. Herring."

Hope turned and smiled. "Hello, Max. Good day?"

"If you're asking about my dives into the online world in order to gain some information about your husband, then the answer is no. I discovered that if you type someone's name into an internet search, you receive over two million returns. I do not have to tell you how long it might take to sift through two million pages on the computer screen."

"And if you limit it to a name and a state?"

"You reduce the number of pages to one million, eight hundred thousand. In my searching, I found out that there's a movie titled Zachariah. It was made in nineteen seventy-one, and it was about two gunfighters and some surreal visions. I also learned that Zachariah is also one of the minor prophets in the Bible. He seems to have focused on the Messiah and the second coming. I have no idea if his prophecies actually mean anything."

"Why did you find out things about Zachariah? That doesn't have anything to do with Doug."

"I have no idea." Max shook his head sadly.

"You're learning the value of being precise in your searches. While the net contains a wealth of information, it takes patience to find something of value. It's very easy to fall down a rabbit hole."

"I agree. I do have patience. After all, I had to wait many, many decades for the solution to my murder. I'm just afraid it will take more decades to glean an answer from the vast web."

"Did you find anything about Doug?"

"I certainly did. I discovered information about his early life, his education, his family." Max smiled at Hope. "But I already knew about the family. I also learned about your husband's work experience and that he'd won several awards for journalistic excellence."

"It's a good start. Maybe you'll be able to figure out what he was working on and what companies he was focusing on."

"I shall endeavor to locate the pertinent information and see what can be seen. And, how was your day, Mrs. Herring?"

"Nothing special, I'm afraid. I think Cori is having an issue with her best friend. Lottie is being less than honest with her mother, and, well, Cori doesn't want to tattle."

"In my day, we had scalawags who never learned to mouth the truth. They were inveterate liars who had to move from place to place, as their lies turned their existence toxic. It was not a recommended way to live."

"I'm aware of the damage lying does. I believe we exist because of the trust we develop between each other. Without trust, our lives become ... difficult."

"Indeed. So, are you going to speak with the girl's mother?"

"I don't want to. I would rather Cori try to help her friend. If that doesn't happen, I think I might be forced to do something depending on how far things go."

"I once had a clerk who told small lies when she was in a pinch. You know, the sort of person who was truthful most of the time. Occasionally, when the truth would besmirch her, she would opt for that lie. I decided I would teach her a lesson. So, one day, I told her she was getting a huge raise, far more than she deserved. She was, of course, very happy. In fact, she spent some of the raise before she received it. At the end of the week, I handed her the usual amount, and she frowned. She wanted to know where her raise was. Well, I informed her bluntly that I had lied to her. She wasn't getting that raise."

"What did she do?"

"She panicked, as she had already spent some of the money. And, she accused me of being cruel and mean. I told her that I lied to her because she often lied to me. While she wasn't trying to be mean, her lies did impact me, just as my lie impacted her. She got the message. She promised never to lie again, and then I gave her enough money to cover her expenses."

"Did she quit lying?"

"She did ... for the most part. Well, she quit lying to me, and that was enough. I don't think she stopped lying altogether. Her husband, I think, expected to hear lies, and I think he was rewarded. People will often give you what you expect of them, whether it be large or small."

"I agree. I hold my students to a high standard, and they generally meet it. They would meet a lower standard, if I offered it." Hope chuckled.

She and Max chatted for a few more minutes before she went down to the kitchen to start dinner. Cori came into the room a few minutes later. She was the salad queen, and she prepared the salad for the spaghetti supper.

Bijou sat on one of the kitchen chairs supervising.

"You found out who killed him, right?" Cori asked.

"Who killed whom?" Hope answered. "Your father?"

"You still think Dad was killed by someone? The police were pretty sure he crashed his car."

"He did crash the car," Hope said quickly. "But, I still wonder if he was run off the road or something."

"Right, but I was actually talking about Maximillian, our ghost from a hundred years ago. Are you sure you found his killer?"

"We've been able to discover the name of the person who we think killed Max. Working a century-old case isn't easy. We can't be a hundred-percent certain that we have the right person since it happened so long ago, but our suspicions were supported by information we got from an insurance company whose records went way back." She gave her daughter some of the details. "Max is satisfied that we've found his killer."

"That's good. I'm glad." Cori chopped some carrots. "Do you think anyone tells the truth on the internet?"

"That's a different question. What makes you ask it?"

"Nothing really. I've just read some stories about people who make friends over the web and then discover their new friend is some kind of weirdo."

"That happens all too often."

"Why?"

"Anonymity. Ask yourself how honest people would be online if no one would ever know who they really were. Think about it. Being totally unseen allows someone to invent an entirely new persona. That teenage girl you're talking to might really be some middle-aged woman, or worse, a middle-aged man. It happens, and it happens because there's no way to verify who the person is who's typing away on the other side of the connection."

"There are pictures and stuff."

"Sure, but anyone can go online and steal someone's picture. It's not difficult at all. And I think I read somewhere that people routinely post pictures that are five to ten years old, because they look younger. I imagine one of the worst things that can happen is to actually meet someone from online. They'll look a whole lot different than what you see on the screen."

"That's creepy."

"It's like the Nigerian prince emails that fill your spam file. The email promises millions of dollars will come your way, if only you invest a thousand dollars now. Of course, there are no millions waiting to be claimed, only a scam that will get the sender a thousand dollars."

"Are there really people who would give over a lot of money like that?"

"When something is too good to be true, it's often untrue. Life doesn't usually offer something for nothing. You can't spend a thousand and get a million in return. If you think about it, the scam is obvious."

"How can you tell when you're texting with the person you think you're texting with?"

"An honest person will talk over the phone or find a way to verify themselves. There's no surefire way to find out the truth so, you have to be careful with everyone. That's true offline also. Just because you're face to face doesn't mean that the person isn't lying to you."

"I don't think I want to leave the house anymore," Cori kidded as she set the salad bowl on the table and then went to get the cat food ready for Bijou.

Hope laughed. "Of course, you do. While you need to be wary, you still have to engage with others. I had a preacher once tell me that if sin came dressed like sin, everyone would be a saint. People are fooled because sin comes looking like candy. That's why it's easy to fall for it."

"Okay, I'm staying a kid. I don't want to grow up."

"Not an option. You have to, and despite the

missteps you'll make, you'll have a wonderful life. I'm certain of that."

Hope held out her arms, and Cori stepped up for a hug.

"You're going to do just fine, Cori. You're far too bright to be taken for a ride."

"Wanna bet?"

They both laughed, and Bijou trilled.

## 4

The next day, when Hope walked into her classroom, she found the principal waiting for her, and her heart dropped. It wasn't a good sign to have the head administrator looking for you.

"Principal Warren," Hope said. "Am I late? Is something wrong?"

"No, no, Hope. Please call me Ardis. I dislike formality. You know that."

"Of course, what can I do for you?"

"I'm making the rounds. You're coming to the Halloween gala, aren't you?"

"I think I replied to the email. I'm planning to come, and I'm bringing my daughter Cori."

"That's great. I'm happy to hear it. I wanted to

make sure. I heard some talk about people not coming on account of Cameron Pender's death."

"I don't see the connection," Hope said.

"I'm the connection."

Ardis Warren was a short woman who still looked to be in good shape. Her suit was freshly ironed and fit well. Hope guessed the woman was in her fifties. She had dyed black hair and wrinkles held in check with anti-aging cream. Her lipstick was pale red, as were her nails, the big ones had the squared off ends that some women favored. Her brown eyes were slightly bloodshot, probably the product of little sleep. School principals answered the phone at all hours. Parents expected no less.

Ardis looked to be comfortable in her job as principal, but Hope had heard some rumblings about her moving up to school superintendent one day. Hope didn't know for sure if that would happen, but it was a logical next move.

"You'll have to explain that," Hope told her. "What do you mean? You're the connection?"

"I'm the drive behind the Halloween gala," Ardis said. "It was my idea. Teachers, parents, and students celebrating each other together. What better time than Halloween? It's not a big holiday like Thanksgiving or Christmas, but just big enough."

Ardis paused for a moment and looked off across the room, as if weighing just how much to say.

"I was the cheerleading coach when Cameron had her ... accident. I wasn't the principal at the time, Wanda Basset was. I was working at one of the district's elementary schools and coaching here. Don't ask me how the accident happened. The team had performed the pyramid a hundred times in practice and at games. Since Cameron was the smallest, she was always on top and she always came off before the others moved. Standard procedure. It was a risky stunt, but not really all that tricky. Anyway, for some reason, the pyramid collapsed early. Cameron fell, landed awkwardly, and broke her neck. It was unbelievably horrible. That she didn't die on the spot was a miracle. But, she did have debilitating injuries."

"What a terrible, tragic accident."

Ardis went on, "Yes, well, the school had insurance, and the parents signed all the waivers. Still, there was a lawsuit and some bad blood. In the end, the parents ended up with a trust fund for Cameron's care. It was enough for the medical expenses, although no one was going to get rich."

"I don't see why people would avoid the gala

because of an accident that happened several years ago."

"People don't forgive or forget readily. I know there are some who will remember the accident and will always blame me for Cameron's death. And, believe me, I was beginning to think I was past that. But I'm not. I doubt I ever will be. So, with that in mind, I wanted to make sure as many teachers and students would attend the Halloween bash."

"I think you'll be surprised. The students and parents who were here when the accident occurred have moved on. The new group of teachers and staff doesn't have that memory. I think attendance will be just fine."

Ardis looked down at the floor. "You know, when I was a cheerleader, we did the pyramid all the time. If you can believe it, I was the little pixie at the top, waving to the cheers. We did that trick every game and never had a problem. I probably shouldn't have taught it to the squad when I was coaching. How I wish I hadn't."

"Accidents happen and we have to move on." Hope stopped, suddenly remembering how difficult it had been for her when Doug died. Her face clouded. Moving on was the last thing she'd wanted to do. If she hadn't had Cori, she might have simply stopped living for a while ... maybe forever.

"Are you all right?" Ardis asked.

"Yes," Hope answered softly. "I lost my husband in an accident. It isn't that easy to move on after a tragedy. So, I sort of know what you're going through."

"Oh, I'm so sorry. I didn't know. Please forgive me?"

"There's nothing to forgive. Like I said, when bad things happen, we have to pluck up our courage and move forward. In my case, I moved all the way to North Carolina from Ohio. So, I ran away a bit faster than most."

"Someday, we'll have a glass of wine, and you can tell me all about it."

Hope nodded. "I'll take you up on that."

With a smile, a really good smile, and a squeeze of Hope's hand, Ardis hurried out the door. Hope guessed there were other teachers to see, to encourage. Ardis was a good principal. She managed by walking about, being seen, interacting with the staff. If someone needed her, she was there. Hope couldn't ask for anything more than that.

"Good morning, Mrs. Herring."

Hope turned. "Good morning, Danielle. How are you today?"

"I'm fine."

Hope was used to the one-word answers she received from most of her students. They weren't in the habit of carrying on conversations, at least, not with teachers. Sitting down at her desk, she pulled the quizzes from the day before from her briefcase. Some of the students would be happy with their grades, and some wouldn't be. That was the way it went. When Hope had been in high school, she had a math teacher who handed out test results by grade. The person who received the highest grade got his or her test first, and, so on, down the line, until the last test was handed out.

Hope had never been the last one to claim a test. Neither was she ever the first one to get hers back. But, she was anxious every time the tests came back. At the time, she thought the practice was horribly embarrassing and unfair. As a teacher, she never handed out the tests in numerical order. She didn't want her kids to feel that kind of sting.

Hope didn't think about Ardis Warren until she was driving home with Cori in the seat next to her. She couldn't help but wonder how much the injury and death of Cameron Pender weighed on the woman. More than Ardis was willing to admit, Hope guessed, enough to cause Ardis to poll her teachers about the Halloween gala. The accident had stayed with the principal, and probably would for a long time.

"Hey, Mom, what is the only bird that can fly backward?"

Hope thought a moment. "I don't know. How many snakes can crawl backward?"

"Well, I don't know about the snakes, but the only bird is the hummingbird. They fly backward from flowers. Are there really any snakes that can crawl backward?"

"I don't know. It would be something to look up. Might make for an interesting fact."

"No way. I'm not going to sound like some nerd, telling people about snakes."

"Do nerds like snakes?"

"Duh, that's like one of their favorite topics. Snakes and spiders. Why is it that nerds think girls are interested in those icky things?"

"They're just trying to get noticed. They don't really care if they're not liked."

"What are you talking about? Not being liked is the worst thing possible."

"Think again, Cori. The worst thing is to be

ignored, unnoticed. Nerds are pretty sure they're not going to be noticed in school. They're smart, but smart isn't important to girls. Good looks and athletics get noticed. But nerds still want attention. So, they talk about snakes and spiders or magic and fantasy, anything to get noticed. Because when someone is noticed, they're being told they're human. We're social animals. We need to be noticed."

"You're not convincing me."

"Think about it. What if you went to school, and no one talked to you? What if no one responded to you, looked at you? How would you like to be that isolated? Not a friend, not even an enemy. How would you feel?"

Hope waited a moment for Cori to consider the question.

"You might be right," Cori admitted. "I would hate to have to talk to myself all day. Not that I'm not a brilliant talker. We both know that I am, and I can have the most satisfying conversations with myself. But I prefer not to, because, well, because. Others should benefit from my insights."

"Please, Cori, spare me," Hope laughed. "No, wait, don't spare me. Give me an example of that brilliance."

"Oh, sure, now you want to benefit from my advanced thinking. Tell me why I should share."

"I thought so. All that talk about brilliance was so much balderdash."

"What? How about that essay I wrote last week? Didn't you say it was positively sensational?"

"I believe my comments included the fact that there were errors, and the essay needed to be rewritten."

"Oh, yes, that. That was just some editing. The idea, the construction, those were genius."

"It was an essay about a dog."

"Not any dog. Our dog, the dog that kept us company for years. That was the dog that saved my life."

"Saved your life?"

"Remember when it grabbed onto my coat and kept me from stumbling into the street in front of a car?"

"The car was a half block away."

"But speeding, remember? Speeding."

"And the dog was trying to get you to play. It was hardly trying to save your life."

"So, you say. I remember it differently. I remember that dog became Lassie, saving the little girl from certain death. I wrote a dizzying essay."

Hope laughed again. "How can I argue with a dizzying work?"

"You can't. Voila."

Hope smiled all the way home.

Before starting dinner, Hope went up to the attic office where she looked at her email and waited for Max to appear. She didn't have to wait long.

"Good evening, Mrs. Herring."

Hope smiled at the ghost who had become her friend. "Hello, Max. How was the internet surfing today?"

"As frustrating as ever. Have you ever heard of Ellery Queen?"

## 5

Hope smiled. "I have. Why do you ask?"

"Well, to be straightforward, I was wondering if you might contact Mr. Queen and perhaps persuade him to help us in our investigation of your husband's death."

"Help us?"

"Oh, I know it's a long shot, and well, I wouldn't expect Mr. Queen to just drop everything he's doing in order to aid us, but I suspect he might be able to shed some much-needed light on the predicament."

"I'm sorry, Max, but you do realize that Ellery Queen doesn't actually exist?"

"No? He doesn't? But, I read several fascinating stories where he solved some rather dastardly mysteries."

"They were just stories, Max. Ellery Queen is a character in books and stories and has been around for decades. In fact, the authors of those stories are dead, too."

"I feel like such an idiot. I thought ... I thought if we could enlist some expert help ... I have been a fool, Mrs. Herring. I hope you can forgive me."

"There is nothing to forgive. Believe me, I would love to have Ellery Queen on the case, along with Perry Mason, Hercule Poirot, Miss Marple, and Sherlock Holmes. We could certainly benefit from their skills."

"But, they are all fictional?"

Hope nodded. "You will find the web filled with detective stories. In most cases, those famous detectives will be characters in a book. They can't come to our aid. The writers who invented those characters might be able to help, but many of them are deceased. We're on our own, Max. Sorry about that."

Max smiled, a tired smile. "I must design a new plan for using the vast resources of the web to our benefit. I trust all is well with you and Cori?"

"We're fine, Max. We're preparing for a Halloween gala at school. But, that won't stop us from working on the case."

"Indeed. I hope to be of help in solving the

*Murder and Deception*

mystery of your husband's accident. For now, I will leave you to your work."

Max faded away, leaving Hope a bit saddened. He had been so enthusiastic about contacting a fictional detective. She wished that they could drop into that fictional world and enlist the services of the best minds ever directed toward crime, but that wasn't to be.

Hope remembered that, as a young girl, she had been fascinated by mysteries. She had read Nancy Drew books, and she envisioned herself as some sort of sleuth. That she had never actually run into a murder didn't faze her. She was ready to solve any death that arrived on her doorstep. As an adult, she still enjoyed a good mystery book or movie. She marveled at the mental powers of master detectives. Her brain didn't work nearly so well. That was the lure of the mystery. How could she mimic what she read or saw?

She couldn't.

Well, she couldn't be like those characters, but she could help the police solve the cases that popped up in Castle Park. She liked being involved. Her goal was to avoid putting herself or Cori at risk, although that didn't always work out the way she wanted.

That had been one of the positive aspects of working on Max's murder. The killer had been dead for many years ... the murderer wasn't going to come after Hope. Did the ghosts of killers ever return to keep their murders from being solved? She would have to ask Max.

"How is the witch costume coming along?" Hope asked her daughter, as she stirred the tomato soup.

"I was wondering if there was such a thing as a white witch," Cori answered. She was busily chopping up carrots and celery for the salad. Bijou was in her usual seat watching the proceedings.

"A white witch? Such as?"

"Glenda in the Wizard of Oz. She was a good witch, and well, she wore that incredible dress."

"I suppose you could go as Glenda, but I'm not sure white witches are a thing. Might be cool to fix up a costume, though."

"Yeah, I was thinking that. But then, who would even recognize a white witch? I don't know of any stories where they exist."

"Doesn't mean you can't be the first." Hope added some chopped onion to the sauce.

"It's just an idea. All the kids would probably laugh at me."

"Would you really mind if they laughed at you?"

Cori frowned and her eyes narrowed. "Who wants to be laughed at? I certainly don't."

"There are many people in history who were laughed at for their ideas. In fact, most inventors had to accept a lot of criticism and flack, but they continued with their experiments and inventions. Being laughed at might really be a mark of genius. If we're not laughed at, maybe we're not thinking large enough."

"Thanks, but no thanks. I'll stick with that old black hat and dress witch thing. Isn't there some sort of Asian saying about a nail and a hammer?"

"It's Japanese, and it's something like the nail that sticks up gets hammered."

"Which means that if you're sticking out, you get beaten down, right?" Cori eyed her mother.

"That's the concept, yes."

"I'll pass on that."

"I think sticking out in a crowd is a good thing."

"Yeah, right." Cori shook her head.

"Do me a favor. Tomorrow, when you're in class, take a look around. Notice how many kids wear something that makes them different from all the others. It might be a streak of pink hair, or black lipstick, or purple jeans, something that signifies their singularity. Everyone wants to be special."

"We should have uniforms. Then, we wouldn't have to worry about wearing the right clothes."

"Uniforms only make it more difficult to stand out. Students still want to be different. Tomorrow, look around. You'll see."

After dinner, Hope spent a few minutes deciding on her own costume for the Halloween gala. If Cori was going to dress up as a witch, maybe she could go as a zombie? The idea struck her as doable, especially if she could find a zombie costume online—a cheap zombie costume. She retreated to her office and started her search.

The first page of the results featured zombie brides and zombie homecoming queens and zombie prom queens and even a zombie teacher. Now, that sounded perfect for the gala. What could be scarier than a zombie teacher? She ordered the costume which would arrive in plenty of time.

In her email, Hope ran across a request from Lottie's mother. Could Lottie ride to school tomorrow with her and Cori? Hope replied to say they would be happy to take Lottie with them.

"Hey," Hope said, as she kissed Cori good night. "Remind me to pick up Lottie in the morning. We're giving her a ride to school."

"Sure. Mom, do you think it's smart to believe what you read online?"

"It depends. Some articles are just fine. Others are nothing more than lies and trash. Why?"

"I think some people believe everything they read. That's not right."

"I'll share a little story. I once met a man who had a mystery to solve. So, he started an online search for help. You know, you look up places and people and things. Well, he came across Ellery Queen."

"Who's Ellery Queen?"

"He's a fictional character who was quite successful in solving difficult murders. Well, this man wanted to contact Ellery Queen and get his help."

"Isn't that like trying to hire Sherlock Holmes?"

"Exactly. It can't be done. In fact, you can't hire Conan Doyle either because he's dead. That's not the point, though. The point is that you have to take everything you read online with some skepticism. Or else, you'll go looking for Ellery Queen."

"I get you." Cori leaned back against the pillows next to her headboard.

"Good," Hope said. "When in doubt, dig a little

deeper into what you're reading or ask someone who will know. Maybe even a parent?"

"Yuck, who would ask their parents to help with internet stuff? They're too old."

"Hah! Parents know a great deal about a great deal. Don't forget that."

"Right." Cori smiled. "I've been spending time in your attic office when you're not using it. I've been talking to Max a lot. He's been telling me about how things were back in his time."

"Max is a nice man. I enjoy talking with him, too." Hope eyed her daughter. "You don't mind having a ghost in the house?"

"Not one bit. Everyone should have one. It's so cool. I really like him. He's a human being, just one who's in a different stage of life. Or maybe I should say *existence*." Cori looked thoughtful. "Talking to Max and getting to know him makes me feel … I don't know. I'm not really afraid of dying anymore."

Hope gently brushed a strand of hair from Cori's forehead. "I know what you mean," she whispered.

∽

The next morning, the first thing Hope noticed about Lottie was her hair. It was frizzy and uncombed, sticking out at all angles, as if she had grabbed some sort of electrical device while standing in a puddle of water. The teen climbed into the SUV and traded hand slaps with Cori.

Then, they launched into a slang-ridden conversation about celebrities from TV and the web. Hope didn't try to keep up. The general gist was a rehash of what was popular, which Hope didn't need to know. She guessed that this morning's topic of choice would change by afternoon. The online world morphed from one thing to another in a matter of seconds. That person who everyone loved at breakfast was taboo by dinner. She was not going to get involved with any of that.

Hope half expected Ardis Warren to be waiting in her classroom. She was wrong, but not disappointed since she had no desire to greet the principal on a daily basis. What she found on her desk was a poster featuring a ghost, a witch, and an angel. The poster advertised the Halloween gala. Hope thought the advertising was a bit over the top.

Did they really need to gin up attendance? She supposed so. Ardis wasn't taking any chances. Hope taped the poster to the whiteboard, where everyone could see it. If Ardis wandered past, she would spot the poster and would think positive thoughts about Hope.

"Good morning, Mrs. Herring."

"Good morning, Danielle."

"Nice poster."

"Yes, it is. Are you going to the gala?"

"I don't think so."

"Why not?"

Danielle shrugged.

"You might reconsider. After all, a costume is a chance to become someone else for an hour or two."

"Is that a good thing?"

"It could be a fun thing. Call it an experiment. Want to be a prom queen? Want to be an elf or a fairy? How about an ogre? You can be whatever you want. And if you wear a mask, people might not even recognize you."

Danielle half smiled. "I could be anything. That might be fun."

"Of course."

"Put on a hockey mask and be the killer from Friday the thirteenth?" Danielle asked.

"Well, that might be a little gruesome, but I don't see why not. Just make sure the knife is made of rubber."

Danielle chuckled. "Yeah, I'll do that."

The morning passed quickly. The students seemed energized by the poster. It seemed that most planned to attend, which was a good thing for both the school and Ardis. Then, Hope got the call.

Cori felt sick.

Hope knew how she would spend her lunch break.

## 6

Since Cori attended the other middle school in town, Hope had to drive the mile that separated the two different schools. She used her card to get access and headed for the nurse's office. Halfway down the hall, she ran into Lottie.

The girl looked like Lottie, but only slightly.

If Hope hadn't seen her hair, she never would have recognized the girl coming toward her. Because the Lottie who was attending classes wasn't at all like the girl who had climbed out of Hope's SUV. This girl wore a mini-skirt, a skirt so short it would be hard to sit modestly. She wore lime green lipstick, accented by lime green mascara and fake eyelashes. A fake mole graced one cheek, and a fake tattoo of a star was on the other. Lottie's top featured a plunging V neckline that would have revealed a lot of cleavage, had she possessed any. In any case, she looked like some cheap vamp from a low-grade movie.

"Lottie?" Hope asked in disbelief.

Lottie looked over, but said absolutely nothing. She just walked on past, as if she hadn't heard or didn't know the woman who had said her name.

In a way, Hope was stunned. When had Lottie transformed from the girl in the SUV to the vamp in the hall? As she entered the nurse's office, she knew Cori had some explaining to do.

Cori was feverish, with a little cough and some sniffles. Hope wasn't worried, as it was probably just a cold. Schools were often like petri dishes. They nourished germs that infected students, teachers, and parents. There was nothing to be done about it. The administration told sick people to stay home, but when parents worked, they often viewed the school as a sort of care facility. The children would find support, until someone had to take them home.

"All right," Hope said, as they drove home. "What's up with Lottie?"

"What do you mean? My head hurts." Cori sat slumped against the passenger door.

"It's most likely a sinus headache. A little acetaminophen and you'll feel better. I mean, I ran into Lottie in the hall, and she was not the teen I dropped off this morning."

"Oh."

Hope waited for more, knowing that Cori was trying to walk the tightrope between telling too much and telling too little.

"Come on," Hope said. "I don't have time for twenty questions. What gives with Lottie?"

"She ... she's changed."

"I can see that. Keep going."

"She wants to be different, so she's started doing stuff. Her mother doesn't like it, so Lottie has to do it at school."

"Do what at school?"

"You saw her."

"I saw a skirt that was far too short and green lips and eyelids and a shirt that was meant for someone a lot older than her. How did she manage that?"

"In the bathroom, before class. She has an extra outfit in her backpack, and she changes as soon as she gets there. She does the lipstick and stuff there, too."

"The fake star tattoo?"

"That, too. She wants to look older and sexier. I think you can see that."

"Why?"

Cori shrugged.

"Does she have a boyfriend or something?"

"Not that I know of. She likes to flirt, though. She tells the cute boys that they have what turns her on."

Hope was appalled to hear this news. "What's come over her?"

"I don't know. When she gets home, she hides all her stuff."

"So, her parents don't know what's going on?"

"No, and you can't tell them."

"Cori...."

"You can't say anything because then Lottie will know that I told you, and she'll hate me for that."

"She's walking the wrong path."

"I know. I told her that very same thing. She won't listen."

"She's listening to someone. Do you know who it is?"

Cori lifted her painful head. "Why do you think she's listening to someone?"

"Because she wouldn't be doing all this stuff on her own. At least, I don't think she would. Is she big into social media?"

"Yeah."

"Come on, what sites does she frequent?"

"You know, Facebook, Tik-Tok, Twitter, Instagram."

"Does she spend a lot of time there?"

"Yeah."

Hope parked and shut off the engine. "I'll watch you go inside. Take some acetaminophen and go to sleep. I'll wake you when I come home. If you need something, call me. I have to get back to class."

"You're not going to stay with me?"

"You'll be safe. Max is in the house. He'll watch over you. Just try to sleep. That's the best thing for you right now."

"I could be dying."

"You're not dying. You have a cold, a viral infection. That's all. You'll be fine in a day or two."

"If I lapse into a coma, you'll be sorry."

"Actually, I'd be flabbergasted. Now, go. I won't call because that will wake you. So, just sleep. Max will make sure you're safe. I'll check on you when I come home."

Cori opened the passenger side door. "You're not going to rat out Lottie, are you?"

"We'll talk about that later. Go, now. Tell Max that you aren't feeling well so he knows why you're at home."

Hope watched Cori trudge across the porch and

into the house. She knew Max was there to watch over her daughter. He'd helped protect them in the past. In a pinch, Max might be able to call Hope, if Cori needed attention. But, the teen wasn't going to need attention. She would survive the cold easily. Children usually did. Nature had made them sturdy enough to weather common illnesses. That ensured the survival of the species. Old people might succumb to small bugs while children just shrugged them off.

Hope managed to forget about Lottie until the last thirty minutes of her school day, which her students could use for reading or studying, they simply couldn't talk or sleep in the last half hour of the school day. While they did their best to avoid learning, she wondered what she should do about Lottie.

It was clear to Hope that the teen needed some guidance. The girl had drifted way past simply wanting to be noticed. She had jumped the fence and opted for notoriety. She was hardly the young girl she used to be. More than that, she probably knew it was wrong. If she thought it was acceptable, she wouldn't have to hide it ... she would dress at home and plant a green kiss on her mother's cheek. Worse, her mother didn't know and neither did her father. They were ignorant, and that couldn't continue. Someone would have to tell them.

Would that someone have to be Hope? Her heart sank.

She sat back to think for a few moments, considering what was really happening. First, was Lottie harming herself or anyone else?

No, Hope didn't believe there was harm involved. It wasn't as if she was doing drugs or smoking. Hope didn't think Lottie was smoking or vaping or drinking. She knew of students who had started drinking alcohol in elementary school, and those kids rarely finished high school. So, Lottie had not adopted habits that would ruin her life—not yet anyway.

Hope didn't see where the girl's actions hurt anyone else either. Some adults might be stunned or disgusted, but they weren't being harmed.

So, what was Lottie doing that needed to be changed?

Well, the exhibitionism was obvious and inappropriate, and Hope was surprised the principal hadn't stepped forward to correct the issue. Of course, Lottie might be adept at hiding from the powers that be. Her teachers knew though. But some teachers could be less than proactive, unless the student's performance was affected. They assumed the parents knew and thus, had approved the behavior. It wasn't an unreasonable stance to take. Since Lottie was changing her clothes at school, Hope was pretty sure her parents didn't know what she was doing.

Again, was it Hope's duty to inform the parents?

The answer was not cut and dried. Someone needed to tell them. That seemed obvious. How long before Lottie tried something stupid? How long before she paid for a real tattoo? How long before she started hanging out with those boys who possessed what turned her on? The path was well trodden. Lottie was straying off the safe path and into the gray ash heap of damaged lives. She hadn't done anything outlandish yet. She hadn't rushed headlong into drugs or alcohol, but she had veered away from what Hope considered a viable avenue. She needed help.

Help.

That was the operative word. Lottie didn't need a lecture and she wouldn't listen anyway. She didn't need discipline or grounding or anything like that. Punishment probably would only make matters worse. But, she did need help and Hope could offer it. That made sense. Hope could offer a different path to follow. In all probability, Lottie would reject all suggestions, since she appeared to be having fun with her new persona. Why would she change? But, Hope needed to try.

Cori was asleep when Hope walked into the bedroom. Bijou was curled up next to her. Automatically, she felt her daughter's forehead and detected a slight fever, but nothing to rock the boat. Of course, the touch woke Cori, who didn't even open her eyes.

"I'm dying," Cori mumbled while reaching out to stroke the cat.

"You're not dying," Hope replied.

"If I don't survive, you can offer my body to science so they can learn what killed me."

"You'll survive. Quit being a drama queen. You're lucky I won't make you do homework."

"Homework? Are you kidding? I'm hours away from the grave, and you want me to do homework?"

"Just go back to sleep. I'll wake you for dinner."

"I don't think I can eat."

"Chicken soup and some more meds might help."

"Chicken noodle soup."

"Of course. And, Cori, despite what you may think, I do love you. I will do everything I can to make this little hiccup more comfortable."

"Thank you, Mom. Later, I'll try to write out my last words, so you can remember me after I'm gone."

"I'll tell you what, save that last testament for tomorrow. The closer you are to the end, the more real you can be."

"Yes, yes, that makes sense. After I die, I'll come back as a ghost and hang out with Max all the time."

Hope smiled and rolled her eyes. "Go to sleep."

Leaving the room, she wondered just when her daughter had learned how to talk like some soap opera actress. Not that it mattered. When Cori was over the cold, she would laugh at all her dying talk.

Hope had just entered the office, when she heard Max.

"I do hope Cori is all right, Mrs. Herring. I kept an eye on her while you were at school. She was resting comfortably all afternoon. Bijou kept an eye on her as well."

"Thank you, Max." Hope turned around and gasped. For the first time since she had met him, he wasn't in his funeral attire.

"Do you like it?" Max asked, with a smile.

# 7

"I ... I don't know what to say," Hope replied.

Max smiled. Dressed in a pink leisure suit from the 1970s, he looked like some sort of throwback peach or lobster. To Hope, he looked utterly ridiculous, but she knew better than to say so.

"Where did you get it?" Hope's eyes were still wide as she took in the sight of the ghost's strange clothing.

"I discovered this online," Max said. "It struck me as just the sort of thing I needed to liven up my life. After all, I've stayed in that black burial suit for longer than I care to remember. With a bit of help from another ghost, I learned that I could dress in any way I wanted, as long as I had a picture to copy. I simply stare at the picture, and like magic, I'm wearing it. I believe this is called a leisure suit, which suits me. I am a man with nothing but leisure to exploit. Do you remember these suits?"

"I do, but they predate me. They were quite popular at one time."

"As they should be. Lots of room and they stretch. Wonderful creation. We did not have stretch clothing while I was alive. How do you like the shirt?"

He pulled apart the suit coat to reveal a floral shirt with a huge collar, something from Hawaii, by all accounts.

"Very colorful," Hope said. "You found this online?"

"Oh yes. You know all your talk with Cori about costumes got me thinking. I have been saddled with my old suit for a hundred years. I needed a tonic to settle my mind and rejuvenate my desire to solve your husband's case. This is precisely the change I was looking for. And these boots." He held up one foot, which was covered in a white boot. "Aren't they simply fabulous. No one had these in my day. I believe I'm positively modern."

Hope was not about to tell Max that he was still more than a few decades short of "modern," but he had made a major leap. He had landed in the disco rage, and that was encouraging. She wondered if he would take up dancing next.

"You do look great," Hope said.

"My only regret is that I have no place to go so I could show off this attire."

"You have an audience of one. And when Cori gets better, you'll have an audience of two. Three, if you count Bijou." Hope smiled. "Bravo to the new clothes."

Max smiled and bowed. "I hope you don't mind me using my computer time to research clothing. Although, I didn't start with the goal of finding a new outfit. I was researching detectives, hoping to learn techniques that would allow me to use on the case, when I happened upon a detective named Magnum. Do you remember him? I believed he played the role on stage."

"TV," Hope replied. "And, that was before me also."

"No mind. He wore these sorts of clothes. I was intrigued, so I started researching suits. When I found this, well, as you can see it is positively gay."

Hope laughed.

"What do you find amusing?" Max asked.

"The word 'gay' has acquired a new meaning since your day."

"Oh?"

"Yes, now, it refers to a homosexual."

"What? You're kidding. A gay man is a … that?"

Hope nodded. "That's right."

"Ahh, I recognize your levity, as that word had no such connotation when I was alive. I should perhaps change my vocabulary."

"A good idea. Joyful is a good word."

"Yes, yes, indeed. I am now joyful. I haven't felt so joyful in quite some time. I believe … sincerely believe that I will soon discover some details about Mr. Herring's accident. How can I not, when I'm wearing such a magical suit? I am guaranteed to find what I want."

"I'm sure you will."

"Before I forget, I must tell you that Cori has been asleep since she came home. I do believe her phone rang once, and she answered. I have no idea whom she conversed with, as I do not eavesdrop. However, the conversation was very short. She is still ill, isn't she?"

"She is, but it's nothing more than a cold, I'm sure. Nothing to worry about at the moment. We'll keep watch over her for a day or two. If she gets worse, we'll go to the Urgent Care facility."

"Urgent Care?"

"It's a small medical facility that specializes in injuries and sickness. You know, if you cut yourself or need a prescription for an antibiotic or something. In and out fairly quickly. If you're really sick you go to the hospital."

"Modern conveniences. In my day, the doctor came to you. Even then, there wasn't a great deal they could do. Set broken bones and bleed patients, who probably didn't need the bleeding. Oh, they delivered babies too. That was something."

"That's done in hospitals now, too, for the most part. There are some women who prefer to have the baby at home."

"As was the norm in my day. Well, I shan't keep you any longer. I wanted you to see what I have managed to do with myself and to tell you how your daughter was faring."

"Thank you very much. I feel much better with you here to look after her. Let it be said, also, that you look quite dashing in your new suit. Very Magnum-esque."

Max laughed, which he didn't often do. Then, with a small bow, he faded from view. Hope couldn't help but remember the pink image. She was amazed at how Max had managed to reinvent himself, in a manner of speaking. She guessed that the internet had created yet one more person who would soon be wearing the latest in fashion.

Hope finished her emails and hustled down to the kitchen where she made the chicken noodle soup Cori wanted. She had to admit that the aroma was tantalizing, and, no doubt, cured the common cold immediately. She was about to fix a bowl and take it to Cori, when the teen walked into the kitchen with Bijou following behind. She didn't look awful, but she didn't look great either.

"How are you feeling?" Hope asked.

"I've been better," Cori answered.

"Did you smell the soup? Is that what got you up?"

"Barely, but it still smells great."

"Sit down and eat. I'll get you more pills."

Cori sat as Hope set the bowl on the table.

"Head still hurt?" Hope asked.

"Some, not too bad. I had this weird dream. You were going to tell Lottie's mom about what she's been doing."

"That's not a bad idea, but I don't think I'm going to do that quite yet."

"Are you going to do *something*?"

"I want to talk to Lottie first."

"Oh gosh, not another teachable moment. Haven't we had enough of those?"

"Nope, not until you're married and have children of your own."

"If it takes getting married, then I'll be at the altar before you know it."

"Don't get smart. I think it's the best way to approach the problem, unless you'd rather I go straight to Lottie's parents."

"No, no, if you can talk some sense into Lottie, great. I've tried, but it hasn't helped. I don't think there's any chance that you having a talk with her will make a difference."

"You've already talked to her?"

"She's my friend. Am I supposed to watch her do dumb things?"

"I take it she's not in listening mode at the moment."

"Not a bit. This soup is great. My throat thanks you."

"Your throat is welcome. Have any idea where she's getting these ideas about fashion? I'm pretty sure she didn't dream it up by herself."

"No, she surfs the net for the stuff. I'm not sure where she goes. She won't tell me. Do you need to know?"

"Not really. Maybe, she'll tell us." Hope wanted to change the subject. "Have you decided on your Halloween costume?"

"Witch, black witch. Traditional. Maybe I'll buy a crooked rubber nose or something. You know, make it really ugly."

"That's traditional. Warts and all."

"Warts? That sounds yucky."

When Cori had finished her soup, she went back to bed. Hope didn't try to stop her, even though all the sleep might keep her awake in the middle of the night. Better to sleep now and worry about that later. Her breathing was normal, so she wasn't suffering too much. Hope guessed that Cori would not be going to school the next day. Max would have to keep an eye on things ... Max in his pink leisure suit. That image made Hope smile. Cori would get a kick out of the new suit. The web had lured Max out of his normal dark shell. He was experimenting. Where that might lead, Hope had no idea. She was pretty sure it wouldn't provide the answer to his quest to solve Doug's case. Sheer luck would have to tap Max on the shoulder.

Morning brought no change in Cori's condition so Hope fixed oatmeal and orange juice for her daughter's breakfast and made her promise to call at lunch time. If she needed anything, Hope would fetch it. Before leaving for the day, she met Max in the attic office, and he was still proudly wearing his pink outfit.

"I will see to her," Max said. "Have no worries. I will be ever vigilant."

"Good. She should be fine. She'll probably sleep for a while and then watch TV or use her computer. Either is fine. Don't worry about using my computer. Go ahead and research whatever you want."

"I will be extra careful, and I will keep tabs on her."

"Thank you."

"I am always at your service."

As Hope drove to school, she considered Lottie's secret life. What had made the girl adopt such an over-the-top character? Where would that character lead Lottie? How was Hope going to get her to talk? More importantly, how was Hope going to get her to listen?

"Good morning, Mrs. Herring."

"Good morning, Danielle."

Hope noted the beginning of the school day. She was happy that some things didn't change.

# 8

When Hope arrived home that afternoon, she found Cori out of bed and sipping a Coke in the family room with her laptop open, playing some game Hope had never seen before. Bijou sat next to the girl watching her play.

"Feeling better?" Hope felt Cori's forehead.

"Much better. I'm fine now. Max kept me company when I wasn't sleeping. We had some good talks. I love his pink suit."

"Good, I'm glad. I brought home your homework and classroom work. You can get started when you feel up to it."

"I think I'm having a relapse."

"I was afraid of that, so I guess you'll just have to

wait until tomorrow to taste the Halloween candy I brought home. Sugar is bad for a cold."

"Who said that? Why, that's crazy talk. Sugar is exactly what a cold needs. I'm sure I read that somewhere."

"You mean nowhere. I guess you'll just have to exist on tomato soup and toasted cheese sandwiches."

"Tomato? No one ever eats tomato soup for a cold."

"I have it on the highest recommendation ... unless you're feeling up to doing homework."

"You know I'm just joking, Mom. Of course, I'll do my homework."

"Wise choice."

Max was waiting for Hope when she walked into her office. He still wore his pink suit, which made him look amusing, but Hope wasn't about to tell him that.

"I must apologize first thing, Mrs. Herring," he said. "Somehow, I must have tapped the wrong key and turned on the speakers. They weren't on long, but they did wake Cori and she came up. I'm profoundly sorry that I woke her, but she seems much better today."

"It doesn't matter, Max. Cori told me you kept

her company for most of the day. She enjoys chatting with you. I'm glad we decided to include Cori in our secret. It has worked out well."

"Definitely so. She took the revelation that a ghost lives in the house quite well. I'm pleased I don't have to hide from her any longer."

"As you have seen, she's much better today. She'll go to school tomorrow, and you won't have to babysit, and you can have the run of the place while we're both out of the house."

"I am thankful she's well. Would you mind terribly, if I changed my attire? I have found some rather interesting clothes to try on."

"I have no problem at all, Max. As far as I'm concerned, you can be a trendsetter in ghostly garb."

"Excellent. This era is filled with all manner of dress. When I remember my days of black and white striped suits and starched shirts, I am positively ashamed. Did we have no creativity in those days?"

"You didn't have high-speed looms and synthetic fabrics. Today, you can pretty much design your own cloth."

"Amazing. Well, I'll leave you to your work. Till later."

"Till later."

When Max disappeared, Hope sat down at her

desk and opened her email. She was relieved and happy that Cori got to meet Max. She'd put off the inevitable for too long. Of course, it meant a thousand questions from her daughter. Hope had to have a conversation with her about the rules. Cori couldn't treat Max like her own personal ghost. She had to understand that, for most purposes, Max was human. He had feelings and thoughts, and she needed to remember that. She couldn't go around bragging about the ghost who lived in the attic. Hope knew the teen would have to remember the rules, if the three of them were to live in harmony.

When Hope drifted down to the kitchen to prepare dinner, she was met by Cori, who carried a package.

"It's for you," she said. "Costumes R Us?"

"For the Halloween gala," Hope answered.

"Cool. What is it?"

"I think I'll leave that till the gala. It will be a surprise."

"Oh, come on, Mom, show me. You know I'm going as a witch. What are you going to be?"

"A teacher."

"Funny. What, really? I need to know."

"Need to know? Why?"

"In case, it's totally wrong. I want to be able to

tell everyone that the person in the lame costume is not my mom."

"Funny. For your information, I will not be wearing a 'lame' costume. And, since when did you stop being proud of your mother? I think we've done quite well here, just the two of us."

"If you include almost getting murdered and then getting blown up. Remember Kaboom?"

"That couldn't be helped. We were in the wrong place at the wrong time. Still, we survived, and that's what counts."

"Just promise me that we're no longer in the murder mystery solving business. I don't know how much more I could take."

"We won't go looking for work, Cori. I promise you that."

"So, what's in the package?"

Hope laughed. "A surprise."

That night, while she was working on the spreadsheet she kept for grading purposes, Max appeared. True to his word, he had changed clothes. He wore a white Nehru jacket, jodhpurs, and knee-high boots. He looked like something from British colonial times in India. Hope fought the urge to laugh.

"How do you like it?" Max asked.

"Stylish," Hope answered. "You're branching out."

"I am indeed. I find changing clothes to be invigorating and freeing. There is an energy in new clothing that I never knew existed when I was alive. That probably sounds self-serving, but it's true. If clothes make the man, then new clothes make a new man. How is that for a bit of optimism?"

"I believe you're right. The easiest way to adopt a new attitude is to adopt a new suit."

"Thanks to your computer, I can visit any place in the world, and I can dress the part."

Max disappeared, leaving Hope tickled. She preferred this manic, enthusiastic Max over the gray, dour man she had first encountered. It was as if he were taking a vacation from his single-minded pursuit of Doug's death. They had only recently solved the ghost's murder. It was good for Max to take a break from investigating serious subjects. He needed to relax, and it seems he was doing so. And that was a welcome change.

Hope's old routine returned the next day. Cori was well, and school was ... school. But Max was the new Max.

She had tried on her zombie costume and was pleased with the result. She'd also bought a ghoulish mask that hid her face. Cori wouldn't be embarrassed. Hope shoved the Lottie situation to the back of her brain, not yet ready to tackle that problem. In a way, she hoped that Lottie would reclaim her senses and become the person she used to be.

Hope would make sure to question Cori about Lottie's actions.

Saturday morning found Hope in the kitchen of the Butter Up Bakery. Her work output would include several Halloween cakes and all those pumpkin cookies Edsel sold by the dozen. Hope was up to her elbows in flour when Edsel poked in her head.

"How's it going?" the woman asked.

Hope smiled at the large, sturdy, older owner of the bakery. Edsel could hold her own in almost all circumstances. She had been around Castle Park for her entire life, and she knew everyone in town—or so it seemed.

"How do you sell so many cookies? I can't bake enough." Hope laughed.

"Halloween seems to get bigger every year," Edsel said. "People decorate and eat like it's Christmas or something."

"I know that's true, but I don't know why. What is

it about ghosts and goblins and witches that fascinates us?"

"We like to be scared," Edsel said. "Oh, we don't like being really scared, truly terrified. But, we like a touch of fear. We like rollercoasters and surprises because we know they won't last. Our hearts beat fast, but they don't stay that way. A bit of a scare is more than enough."

"You're right, Edsel. We like that adrenaline rush. It's the reason people do zip lines and rock climbing. They want their hearts to pump a little faster. They want a shot of energy."

"We are our own worst enemies. You would think we would appreciate a rocking chair and a hot toddy. Instead, we drink strong coffee and look for a tree to climb."

Hope laughed. "Are you going to the Halloween gala tonight?"

Edsel shook her head. "Nope. I'm going to stay home with that hot toddy. You going?"

"I'm a teacher. It's pretty much a command performance, so yes, I am."

"Well, I'm sure you'll have a good time. I've overheard more than one customer say they're looking forward to the event."

"That's great for the school and for Ardis, our

principal. The gala is her idea."

"I'm sure you all will have a great time. When you leave today, be sure you take a dozen cookies home for you and Cori. That girl is too skinny."

Before Hope could protest, Edsel was back out at the front of the bakery.

Cori was definitely not too skinny, she was athletic and healthy. Hope did remember to take home the cookies. She found Cori on her tablet computer, chatting with Lottie.

Hope could have taken the opportunity to arrange a meeting with Lottie, but she didn't want to get into that. She wanted a quiet afternoon that led to a memorable party.

"This cookie is great," Cori said. She sat at the kitchen table, tablet and soda beside her.

"It should be. I certainly baked enough of them to get it right." Hope kidded as she made herself a cup of tea.

"Are you going to tell me about your costume?"

Hope shook her head. "Not until we're ready to walk out the door."

"That's all right. I have come to the conclusion that I can pick out the person with the best costume and claim she's my mom."

Hope frowned. "You're going to dump me for some Frankenstein or something?"

"The beauty of a masked party." Cori grinned and took another bite of her cookie.

"That prerogative is a two-way street. I can say the smart, cheerful, little princess is my daughter."

One of Cori's eyebrows raised. "You wouldn't."

"You never know."

Hope left Cori in the kitchen and went up to her office where she considered pulling up one of Doug's files, but those always seemed to be downers. She didn't want to feel sad before the gala. Instead, she processed her email and visited some of her favorite sites until it was time to get ready.

Looking at her costume and mask laid out on the bed, Hope grinned. It was going to be a surprising night. She was sure of that.

How surprising? She had no idea.

# 9

Hope knew her costume was a hit when she showed herself to Max. Even without the mask, she looked to be an authentic zombie.

Max, in his fresh new clothes, stared at her. "I'm sorry, Mrs. Herring, but I am at a loss. What sort of monster are you to be?"

"A zombie."

"A zombie? I'm afraid I am unfamiliar with that sort of being."

"Oh, that's right, you weren't alive when zombies became popular. I think that occurred in the fifties and sixties. Zombies are reanimated dead who feast on the brains of the living. They are slow moving and nearly indestructible. Very difficult to kill.

They're created by being attacked by another zombie. They always seem to have wounds and blood. Of course, as reanimated, they are grayish."

"Yes, because of the lack of warm blood. I see. Well, you fit the description quite nicely. I, for one, would hate to meet you in a dark alley."

"That's the desired effect. I'm glad you approve."

"Indeed, I do. You would be a popular zombie, if they really existed." Suddenly, Max looked worried. "They don't exist, do they?"

"No, there are no zombies and there are no vampires. You've never run into a vampire, have you?"

"I can honestly tell you that there are no vampire ghosts … as far as I know."

"That's good to hear. All right, I must go. I think this is going to be a very good night for the school. I plan to have fun, and I'm certain Cori will have a ball, since she's feeling so much better now."

"Enjoy the evening. I would be lying if I said I didn't envy you. I wish I could be one of the many in attendance."

"If you decide to leave the house and not disappear forever, then you could join me at the event."

"I would like nothing better, but it might be too

far for me to wander. I do want to be able to return to the house. I'll keep my wanderings close to home."

―

Cori looked exactly like an evil witch, complete with crooked nose and warts. Her costume, while not original, was certainly impressive.

"Oooh," Cori said, "you're a zombie. Cool."

"A zombie teacher," Hope said. "Your worst nightmare."

"Not necessarily. If you eat a student's brain, he has an excuse to do poorly on tests."

"If I had to eat student brains, I'd probably starve to death."

"Very funny. Remind me to laugh."

"Can't take a joke? Never mind. Let's get going."

The school parking lot was over half filled, which pleased Hope. Ardis had wanted a good turnout, and that was happening.

"The gym will be crowded," Cori said.

"The way it should be. A very intimate affair."

"Intimate?" Cori scrunched up her face. "How could a crowded gym be intimate?"

"Think about it. If the party is small, everyone notices when someone disappears, even for a few minutes. But in a crowd, people can disappear for long stretches and not be missed."

"I never thought of it that way. I can slip out and drink a beer, and everyone will think I'm just across the room."

"Exactly, but don't even consider such a thing. I would notice later, and you would be in a heap of trouble."

"I know, which is why I won't do anything that stupid. I'll just observe and fill my brain with items for my diary."

"You keep a diary?"

"It's more of a journal, and it's online. There are a bunch of apps and sites for journaling."

"Fair enough. I don't think I want to read it."

"Right, Mom. Ignorance is bliss."

Hope laughed. "If that's the case, some people I know should be euphoric." She put on her mask as she walked across the parking lot.

"I have to say, that's one great costume," Cori said. "In a year or two, I'm going to borrow it."

"You're welcome to it. Zombies are popular around Halloween."

The table in front of the gym was staffed by three

blind mice. Hope knew they were teachers, and she could guess who they were. Their costumes and masks were impeccable, complete with dark glasses and red-tipped canes. The mice checked off Hope's and Cori's names and stamped the back of their hands. Partiers could step out and reenter, mainly because the restrooms were down the hall from the gym.

The gym had been transformed into a graveyard. The stage at one end was filled with fake gravestones that popped up out of a white fog, created by several fog machines. The white wave flowed over the edge, like a fountain of some kind. It didn't fill the gym, as there were too many bodies and too much space, but the stage with its dark shadows was eerie enough. Behind the stones, fake lightning flashed across the backdrop. Cemeteries were bad enough in the dark. A storm made it much worse.

Black and orange streamers crisscrossed the ceiling. On one side, the bleachers had been transformed into a haunted house, with lighted windows filled with ghosts and witches and vampires. Someone had gone to a lot of trouble to provide a mansion straight out of some Gothic novel. As Hope noted the decorations, a wolf howl echoed through the gym. Her heart skipped a beat, even though she knew there were no wolves inside the gym. A black bat darted across the ceiling. A giant spider sat in its web in one corner. All the tropes had been used. Hope was glad she wasn't in some strange building.

"I'm going to find Lottie," Cori said.

"All right, keep your phone on. No leaving without approval, okay?"

"I know. I'm not going anywhere."

While Hope watched Cori head into the throng of costumes, her phone buzzed in her pocket and she took it out to find a text from Luke.

*Have fun at the Halloween dance. Wish I was there with you. How about meeting for breakfast before you go to work at the bakery on Saturday?*

With a warm smile, she texted him back. *Yes! Let's meet for breakfast.*

Looking around at all the people, Hope admired the costumes. While the traditional characters—ghosts, vampires, witches, werewolves—were heavily represented, there were other costumes to be noted. There were several clowns who were spooky, despite their painted smiles. There was a dinosaur with ferocious teeth and a bumblebee with a foot-long stinger. Uncle Sam danced with the Statue of Liberty. The Blues Brothers, black fedoras and sunglasses, stood next to the punch bowl. Hope spotted a lion and a lamb and several elves. One couple had come as peanut butter and jelly. All in all, there was enough fake blood for anyone's tastes, with more than enough ugly masks. Frankenstein roamed stiffly all about the dance floor.

As Hope walked about, she received more than a couple of compliments on her costume. She wasn't the only zombie at the gala, but she was one of the better dressed. Halfway around the perimeter, Hope ran into Ardis who had come as an elf. She made for a cute elf, perhaps one from Santa's workshop.

"Thank you for coming," Ardis smiled widely. "The place is beginning to hop."

"Everyone loves a costume party. I'm amazed by how inventive people can be."

"I know, and I have a favor to ask. Would you help with the best-costume contest? I would like to have a few teachers on the judge's panel. I mean, it will seem more authentic, if it's someone besides me."

"What do I have to do? Go around with a clipboard and rate costumes?"

"No, we don't want to embarrass anyone. It's strictly for people who want to be in the contest. We'll set up in front of the stage and ask all interested parties to come forward. We'll pick the best costume from them."

"That will work. Count me in."

"Thank you so much, Hope. Since you're known for your fairness, no one is going to question the decision."

"Someone will always question the judges, but that's fine. How many judges are you going to recruit?"

"Five. I want each judge to pick out five costumes and rate them from one to five, the best costume getting the most points. We will have two winners, male and female. The costumes with the most points will win."

"What's the prize?"

"The Butter Up Bakery has donated gift cards good for whatever someone might want. And, the two best will reign as king and queen of the cemetery. What do you think?"

"Reign?"

"We will place some chairs in the fog, and they will preside over the festivities...for a few minutes. They will have a dance by themselves, too. It should be a lot of fun."

"It will be. Let me know when it's time."

"I will."

Hope noticed how Ardis stared at a couple not too far away. Marie Antoinette and King Louis appeared to be whispering to each other.

"That's my husband," Ardis frowned. "Chatting up another pretty woman."

"Your husband?"

"There's no fool like an old fool. I have to go rescue her. I'll come back."

Hope watched Ardis slip through the crowd and stop by the king and queen. Would they be part of the judging squad? She knew that the process and the result would not please everyone, but that couldn't be helped. Some egos simply couldn't accept anything but a win. People were people. They didn't get better because it was a holiday.

Hope found some other teachers to chat with, and for the next half hour, she guessed at the identity of the people behind the masks. It was a fun game. The students were, for the most part, easy to spot. The adults, however, were more clever. Some of them had gone to great lengths to not be recognized. Among the most clever were the twins, identical twins.

Tweedledum and Tweedledee.

The two were a couple, and that was as far as Hope could get. She didn't have a clue as to who they might be, or their affiliation with the school. She was to the point of introducing herself, when Ardis appeared.

"Ready?" Ardis asked?

"As ready as I'll ever be."

## 10

Hope joined four other teachers in front of the stage, as Ardis announced the contest. Anyone who wanted to be considered had to move to the front where the judges could evaluate the costumes. Hope had been given a pad and paper, and she was ready to do her job.

The number of contestants was small. Hope guessed that most people were fully aware of their costumes and the possibility of winning against the others. As the monsters and ghouls and princesses lined up, Hope surveyed the field. For her money, Tweedledum and Tweedledee wore the best costumes. They were identical, right down to their heights and shapes. Hope found it impossible to tell them apart. They had gone to some lengths to achieve the image—red propeller hats, oversized white shoes, red-and-white striped socks. Hope wanted to reward that.

Still, there were other costumes that were almost as good. There was an E.T. costume that made Hope laugh and a Ghostbuster outfit that came with a ghost repelling gun of some sort. There was a Mad Hatter and a Willie Wonka and even someone dressed as an FBI agent. In all, the costumes displayed creativity and imagination, which was what she was looking for. She added four more costumes to her list of five and ranked them in order.

Ardis stopped Hope and whispered. "Do not let the Mad Hatter win."

"Why not?"

"He's my son, and if he wins, everyone will think the contest was rigged. Spread the word."

"Got you."

Hope managed to inform the other judges, and that ensured a loss for the Mad Hatter, whose costume was authentic. Too bad.

Ardis collected the notepads and went to the side to tally up the totals. Hope waded through the contestants, looking for Cori and she found her daughter off to one side, talking to Lottie, who wore a conservative nun habit. The costume didn't look like anything Cori had described. Of course, the juxtaposition of nun and witch struck Hope as pure Halloween magic.

"Hey, girls," Hope said, "did you watch the costume contest? Who did you vote for?"

"I liked Willie Wonka," Cori said. "Anyone who owns a chocolate factory is fine with me."

"The people in the propeller hats," Lottie said.

"Tweedledum and Tweedledee?"

"Yeah, those two were like looking in a mirror or something."

"I think so, too. Have any idea who they are?"

The girls shook their heads.

"We'll soon know. I believe the principal is coming to give out the prizes."

Hope and the girls moved to the front of the throng, as Ardis grabbed the mic and smiled.

"We have a winner," Ardis said. "First, I have to commend everyone who came tonight. The judging was fierce, and the final numbers were close. Congratulations to everyone."

Ardis led a round of applause which allowed the students to become a bit raucous. Kids were like that.

"However, we did get a winner, or winners in the

case. Would Tweedledum and Tweedledee step forward?"

Hope watched as the twins walked to the mic and joined Ardis.

"Before I hand out the gift certificates which the Butter Up Bakery was kind enough to donate, I'm going to ask our winners to remove their masks, so we can see who actually won. If you don't mind."

As Hope watched, the twins removed their hats and masks. As soon as they had, there was a group gasp from the crowd.

"What?" Hope asked Cori and Lottie. "What's the problem?"

"We don't know," Cori answered.

Hope look around, noticing the concerned looks, although the couple standing next to Ardis looked perfectly normal. Yet, they'd had an effect on Ardis, too. Her smile was forced, as if she were dealing with people she didn't like.

"What's the problem?" Hope whispered to the baseball player standing next to her.

"Those are the Penders," the player answered.

"Penders?"

"The parents of the cheerleader who broke her neck and died."

"Oh, I see, that does make it awkward, doesn't it."

"Well, yes, since Ardis was the cheerleading coach at the time."

Ardis handed over the gift certificates, led a round of applause, and then rushed away. Hope thought to follow and offer support, but she supposed the principal wanted to be alone. Being reminded of the tragic collapse would knock the legs out from under even the bravest soul.

Instead, Hope grabbed Lottie and Cori and led them onto the dance floor when the music restarted. From there, she watched Tweedledum and Tweedledee sit in their thrones in the middle of the fog laden cemetery. They looked out of place. Who would expect the twins to be king and queen?

At some point in the next half hour, Tweedledum and Tweedledee left the stage. One minute they were there, and the next they were gone. Hope supposed neither wanted to sit in the cold fog for the rest of the night. Cori and Lottie were a hit on the dance floor. Hope stepped back to watch the witch and nun try out their moves. It struck her as funny.

Feeling hot, Hope decided to step outside. She passed one blind mouse, who was still at the table.

"I'll be back," Hope said. "I need some air."

"Take your time," the mouse answered. "I'll be here."

Stepping into the cold parking lot, Hope was happy for the change of temperature. While it was cool, it wasn't frigid. She looked up at the full moon and took a deep breath. It was a pretty night. It was a fun time, too, even if there had been an awkward moment when the Penders won the costume contest. To Hope's eyes, the couple looked as surprised and stricken as Ardis. That was to be expected. She hoped the bad times would pass. After all, Cameron Pender was dead. There was nothing more to argue about.

That was when she noticed the motor.

The running motor.

That struck Hope as odd. She guessed a couple had left the gala to smoke or sneak a drink or something. She thought to let it go, but that sort of behavior was not condoned or appreciated. She decided to find the vehicle and end whatever tryst was happening.

Her walk led her to the teachers' lot. The car in question was at the front, by the door. In fact, it was the principal's slot, reserved for whoever held the position. As soon as Hope reached the point where she could see the car, she knew something was dreadfully wrong. There was a length of hose running from the car's exhaust pipe to the slightly open driver's side window.

"Oh no," Hope whispered and ran to the car.

She tried the door, but it was locked. She knocked on the window and peered into the interior. There was a person slumped over the wheel, but Hope couldn't tell who it was.

Frantically, she ran around the car trying the doors, but they were all locked. She stopped to hammer on one of the windows, but the person inside didn't budge. Knowing she couldn't smash a window with her fist, she pulled out her phone and dialed 911.

"What is your emergency?" the 911 operator asked.

"I'm standing next to a car filled with exhaust. Someone is inside the car, but I can't get in since the doors are locked. Hurry."

"Stay on the line, please."

Hope waited by the side of the car. Within minutes, Detective Derrick Robinson, dressed in an orange prison jumpsuit came running up. Hope had worked with the detective on several cases. She knew the African American man to be competent and brave.

"Who is it?" the detective asked.

"I don't know," Hope answered. "It's the principal's parking spot and car."

"Crap. All right, stand back."

"What are you going to do?"

"Break the window, if I can. We have to get her out of there." He hit the window hard, but not hard enough. "That's not going to work. I'll be right back."

Hope watched Derrick race away. Then, she banged on the car window.

"Ardis! Ardis! Stay awake, Ardis. Help is on the way. Don't fall asleep!"

Hope received no answer or indication that the person inside was awake. She didn't even know for sure if it was Ardis. Still, Hope continued to hammer on the window and call out. It was the only thing she could think to do.

In the distance, Hope heard sirens. Help was coming, but would it arrive in time?

Derrick reappeared, a tire iron in hand.

"Get back," he said again.

Hope stepped to the side and watched as Derrick struck the window, shattering it. He used the tool to clear out the glass and reached inside to unlock the door. In seconds, he had managed to grab the person behind the wheel and pull her free. Even as he laid the woman on the cold pavement, Hope knew who it was.

Ardis.

"Know CPR?" Derrick asked.

"Yes," Hope answered. "All teachers know some lifesaving procedures."

With that, she knelt beside the principal and began chest compressions. Hope could see that Ardis's lips were red, and that was a bad sign. People who died from carbon monoxide often had red lips, as if their blood was trying to escape.

"Stay with us," Hope told Ardis, although she was pretty sure the woman was dead. Still, she had to try.

Derrick ran off to flag down the emergency vehicles. The bright lights and sirens pulled people out of the gym, and they gathered around the scene. Another minute passed before an EMT relieved Hope, taking over the chest compressions. When she stepped back, Cori appeared and stared.

"Is that …?" Cori asked.

"It is," Hope said sadly.

"Is she?"

"I think so." Hope's voice was soft.

Derrick turned off the car engine as several police officers moved the crowd back away from the life-saving activity.

"Where is she?" A man asked frantically.

Hope turned to find King Louis, Ardis's husband rushing up.

"Where's Ardis? Where's my wife?"

Derrick hurried over to the man. "Step back, please. They're working on her. Give them some space."

Right behind the King came the Mad Hatter.

"Oh, no. Is that Mom?" the Hatter asked as he stared at the body on the ground.

"It is," King Louis replied with a sob.

"Is she...?" The Hatter broke down in tears.

"I don't know.

The Mad Hatter joined King Louis at the front of the onlookers. Hope could have told them that Ardis was gone, but that was Derrick's job. She didn't have the heart, and it wasn't her place.

"Can we leave?" Cori asked.

"I'm the one who found her," Hope said. "They'll want to talk to me."

"Okay. I'm going back inside," Cori told her. "It's cold out here."

"I'll come and get you as soon as I can."

As Hope watched Cori walk away, she realized that her daughter had seen far too much death in her short life ... far too much.

"All right," Derrick came over to Hope. "Let's find a place where we can talk."

# 11

Detective Robinson led Hope to the other side of the ambulance and its flashing lights.

"I'll keep this short," the man said. "If I need more, we'll talk tomorrow. What were you doing in the parking lot?"

"The gym was hot and stuffy, and my mask didn't make things any better, so I stepped out."

"All right. And the car?"

"I heard the engine running, and I thought it was two teenagers making out or something. That's not allowed, and I'm a teacher. I've done playground patrol all my working life."

"Go on."

"When I approached the car, I noticed the hose from the exhaust pipe, and, well, we all know what that means. I tried to open the doors, but they were locked. I couldn't find anything to smash the window with, so I called 9-1-1. Then, you appeared, and you know the rest."

"You didn't see anyone else by the car?"

"Not a soul. Not that I was looking. I mean, I did glance about for someone or something that could help, but I didn't spot anything."

"All right. I know the rest. I probably will want to chat more tomorrow, but there's not much to be done tonight. This isn't good, Hope, not good at all. We don't want to lose our community members like this."

"I'll be available. And, I agree. Suicide is an awful thing. Everyone will think that they missed the signs."

"It's always that way."

Hope made her way to the gym where she found Lottie and Cori by the cookie table. She guessed the two had had more than their fair share of pumpkin cookies.

"Ready to go?" Hope asked.

"Yeah," Cori answered.

"Me, too," Lottie said. "Mom just texted me."

"You know, Lottie," Hope said, "I'm thinking of

taking Cori to the mall for a bit of shopping one of these days. Would you like to come along?"

"Sure," Lottie said.

"I'll check with your mother. We'll set a date."

"Great."

Lottie scooted off and Hope and Cori headed for the exit.

"That wasn't cool," Cori said.

"What wasn't cool?"

"Getting Lottie to go shopping with us."

"Why is that?"

"Because you'll use the time to give her a boatload of advice. And, she'll think I was in on it."

"You are."

"No, no, I'm not. I didn't narc on Lottie, and I don't want her to be mad at me."

"I'm afraid she's going to be mad no matter how I manage to get her alone. She might think you put me up to it."

"Unless I'm not there."

"You're going, Cori. It may be uncomfortable, but it's necessary. You're the witness."

"Witness? What witness?"

"When two people have a serious discussion, they should have a witness. Otherwise, it becomes a he-said-she-said situation. No one will know the absolute truth. A witness clarifies things and keeps the other two from lying."

"I'll remember that. Can't you find another witness?"

"You're a natural."

"But I like both of you."

"Precisely. If you disliked one of us, you wouldn't be trustworthy."

"I'm not at all sure I like this."

"You don't have to like it. But, you have to do it."

Outside, they noticed that the emergency vehicles were still parked near Ardis and her car. Hope didn't stare. She was already too involved, for her way of thinking. Husband and son could take care of Ardis now.

At home, Hope spent half an hour un-costuming herself. What had gone on so easily did not come off in the same way. When she was finished, Cori was already in bed with Bijou resting on her chest.

"Worn out?" Hope asked.

"A little." Cori patted the fluffy cat. "It's sad about Principal Warren, isn't it?"

"It's very sad."

"Why would she do that?"

"I don't know." Hope took Cori's hand. "There are going to be days when you're sad and depressed and lonely. No one basks in joy all day, every day. Life doesn't work that way. You may find yourself in an impossible situation. You may not see a way out. You might despair. You know what despair is?"

"I think so. It's when you lose all hope, right?"

"It is indeed. Life can hide the path that will lead you to safety. You must fight despair and melancholy and depression. They're not uncommon. They happen to everyone. Just remember that everyone muddles through the tough parts of life. It's a rollercoaster. You go up, and you go down. There is always an up after a down, and a down after an up. It's crazy, but it's true. When you're down, you look for the next up. Remember that. And it helps to talk to someone. A different perspective might make all the difference in the world."

"The principal must have been really down."

"It happens. If you see it in one of your friends, help them. Find help for them. Don't let them crater."

"I won't."

Hope kissed Cori and left the room. Although she was tired, she decided she had just enough time to wade through her email. She guessed that half the messages would be about Ardis and her death. Hope was going to ignore those. They would be speculation, for the most part, and speculation led to gossip. It was better to not get involved in that.

"Good evening, Mrs. Herring," Max said.

Hope turned to find Max back in his pink suit, which seemed a bit too bright for that night.

"Hello, Max."

"I take it there was a bit of excitement at the school tonight."

"There was. Ardis Warren was found in her car with the engine running and a hose attached to the exhaust."

"Suicide?"

"It would seem so."

"I am very sorry."

"It's sad."

"In my day, suicide was against the law, and it was a dastardly sin. It left everyone diminished. Survivors blamed themselves, even when there was no blame to be laid. Since suicides could not be buried in hallowed ground, a suicide was often described officially as an accident. The family and friends could live with that."

"I understand. People don't want to feel the guilt of not doing something while the deceased was alive."

"Indeed. I shall say a prayer for the deceased. It isn't much, but it is all I can do."

"Thank you, Max. I'll make that known to her family...without exposing your existence."

"No one would believe you anyway."

Hope smiled. "That is true. They would simply label me as someone given to very odd visions and perhaps headed for some sort of hospital, where I would be filled with all manner of drugs."

"In my day, you would have been warehoused in some institution."

"Sometimes, we simply don't know what to do with those who have challenges."

"Well, I will let you get to bed. You look as if you could use the sleep."

"I can. I'll see you tomorrow."

"The pleasure will be mine."

Hope watched the ghost fade away.

The next morning passed without incident. Cori was over her cold and Hope was back in her classroom.

"Good morning, Mrs. Herring."

"Good morning, Danielle. Did I recognize you in a Tweetie Bird costume?"

"That was me. It was cool."

"Yes, it was a good gala."

"You know about Mrs. Warren, right?"

"I do, Danielle. What happened will be covered in the news. If any of the students need to speak with a counselor, I'll give them a pass to go and meet with one of them. For those who stay in class, we'll focus on our activities today."

Danielle moved on to her desk. As the room filled, Hope could make out some of the whisperings. Mrs. Warren had gone "sideways." That was scuttlebutt. She had had one too many disappointments.

The room filled, and the morning announcements began. Only, they weren't read by Ardis. They were read by Elizabeth Scott, the highest-ranking assistant principal. Elizabeth was quick to share the bad news with the school and to invoke a moment of silence in respect for the dead principal. She offered no explanation. The silence was enough. When "arrangements" were known, they would be shared with the school population.

Hope took the opening five minutes to field any questions the students might have—the ones she would be able to answer. They didn't ask much. The death was open and shut. For once, no one asked if Hope was going to solve the death.

There was nothing to solve.

Until Hope received a call from Detective Robinson. He asked her to stay after school ended, so they could ... talk.

## 12

When Detective Robinson walked into the classroom, Hope sent Cori to the library to study. While she trusted Cori to keep a secret, she didn't think her daughter needed to hear any details of Ardis's death. The look on Cori's face showed she would rather stay behind, but Hope ignored her.

The tall, black detective took a seat in one of the front desks, which was decidedly too small for him, but he didn't complain.

"You can have my chair," Hope offered.

"No, no, this is fine. Thank you for meeting with me. Before I start asking questions, I want you to know that the death of Ardis Warren is being investigated as a murder."

"Murder?" Hope's breath got stuck in her throat

for a few seconds. "She didn't die from carbon monoxide poisoning?"

"Oh, she did, but that was because she had been clubbed in the head first and placed in the car."

Hope's vision swam for a moment as the reality of the detective's words sunk in. "Someone hit her and tried to make it look like suicide?"

"It would appear so. According to the medical examiner, the blow to the back of the head was more than enough to knock her unconscious. We're guessing she was placed in the car, then, someone ran the hose and started the engine. She was dead in a matter of minutes."

Hope frowned. "So, they left the key inside?"

"No, the fob was on the ground. They'd locked the car doors. That's why you couldn't get in."

Hope thought about the implications. "It also means that I might have been the one to bop her over the head and place her in the car."

"Yes, I have to add you to the suspect pool, although I don't think you had a motive."

"I didn't. I don't. I simply noticed the car and did what I could."

"Exactly. So, I want you to think back and try to remember if you saw or met anyone in the parking lot."

"No, no, I didn't. I mean, it was dark, so someone might have been lurking nearby. I wouldn't have noticed them. And, once I reached the car, I was focused on getting Ardis out."

"That's understandable. So, let's go back a little. You were inside with the crowd. In fact, from my notes, you were one of the judges for the best costume contest."

"I was. There were some terrific costumes last night."

"I know. Did you see or notice the deceased talking or, perhaps, arguing with anyone?"

"I didn't. I know she was there with her husband and son. She pointed them out to me. But, I didn't see any altercations. Oh, she did refer to her husband as an old fool, for whatever that's worth."

"Who knows? I haven't been able to dig out any motives yet, but I'm sure they'll pop up like daisies once I get started."

"Sometimes, motives need digging out," Hope said. "People hold grudges for a long time."

"I know, and the murder happened at a perfect time. Even if you had spotted someone, chances are that unless the costume was one of a kind, you wouldn't be able to identify the person wearing it."

"That's true. How many ghosts and witches were there last night? Too many to pick out one."

The detective stood. "I'll leave you to your work. If you get any brainstorms, call me."

"I have a question. Did you find any fingerprints?"

"Yes and no. We found a lot of prints on the fob and inside the car, but we haven't sorted them out yet. I'm guessing most of them will belong to the victim or her family members. And, there will probably be some that we can't identify because the owners aren't in any system. Still, we'll run down as many as we can."

"My prints will be on the door handles and windows. Maybe other places outside. I don't recall touching anything inside the car, but then, I was busy. I might have."

"I'll remember that. Have a good evening, Hope."

"You, too."

Hope watched Derrick walk out the door, and she realized that the cordial air between them might soon become chilly. Since she'd found the body, she was a suspect. As a suspect, she would not be privy to the facts and clues the police uncovered. She could hardly expect to solve the murder, even though she had solved murders in the past.

*Murder and Deception*

Would she try to solve it?

She didn't see why not. Solving the case would keep her out of jail and the courtroom. As she packed her briefcase for the drive home, she tried to remember if she had ever had a run-in with Ardis. Was there some sort of motive that someone might try to pin on Hope? Certainly, the two had had differences of opinion as to the school and its curricula, but that was to be expected. Teachers were honor bound to stand up for the education of their students—no matter what the school board said.

She didn't have a motive.

No motive eased her anxiety, but it didn't move her any closer to the truth. She would need a lot of help, if she was to assist the police.

"What was that about?" Cori asked.

Hope slowly pulled out of the school parking lot. While the principal's car had been removed, the space it occupied was surrounded by orange cones and yellow crime tape. The tape fluttered in the wind, some sort of testimonial to the murder. Hope wondered just how long the tape would remain in place. Too long.

"You're going to find out about this soon enough," Hope said. "Principal Warren was murdered."

"Murdered? You're kidding."

"Nope. Someone hit her over the head and knocked her out before she was put in the car. She died of carbon monoxide poisoning, but she was unconscious at the time."

"Ooh, that's so radical. Who did it?"

"Do you think Detective Robinson would question me, if he knew who had committed the crime?"

"Wait, wait, does he think you did it? Because you found the body?"

"That would be the logical connection. I wouldn't be the first killer to call the police to the scene of the crime."

"But, you didn't do it. He must know that. You're always helping him."

"I told him that, and I think he believes me. However, he's thorough. He's not going to cross me off the suspect list until I've been exonerated."

"Well, I know you didn't do it. I'll be a character witness if you need one."

"Well, thanks for the offer, but family members don't make good character witnesses. What would we expect them to say? That their mother or sister or brother are evil and certainly committed the crime?"

"That wouldn't work, would it. All right, I'll start

a crowd-sourcing page and ask people to donate to your defense. You'll need money for the attorneys."

"I haven't been arrested or charged, so I don't need an online money campaign. Save that for later."

"All right, but I'll tell you right now that starting early is much better than starting late. If people think you're guilty, they won't contribute."

"Think about what the police would do, if we started begging for funds before we've been charged? They might conclude that I really am guilty based on my behavior."

"That's crazy. Everyone has the right to go after money."

"True, but setting up the page early would indicate guilt, like fleeing the jurisdiction. People who take off are believed to have committed the crime."

"All right, but we should prepare anyway. We don't have to actually go live until they give you an orange jumpsuit and throw you in jail."

With a smile, Hope said, "Focus on your homework and studies. There will be time enough later, if it comes to that."

"Don't make me say I told you so."

"I won't. By the way, did you talk to Lottie about her problem last night?"

"A little. She's talking to someone online, who's giving her all sorts of goofy ideas."

"Who is it? Did she say?"

"I don't know, and she won't tell me. It's very no-name, if you know what I mean."

"What sort of online person?"

"Sort?"

"You know, older, younger, close by, across the country, around the world. Who is she talking to?"

"I have no idea, but I think it's a woman."

"What makes you think that?"

"Just what Lottie says about dressing and makeup and being sexy. That's girl stuff."

"Probably. Can you find out? I think it would help, if we knew who was chatting with her."

"I can try. You do realize she's my friend? And friends don't betray friends, right? Isn't that what you taught me?"

"Trying to help someone isn't betrayal, although I can see where people might think so. Sometimes, you have to do what's right, even if it means your friend won't like you for a while."

Cori scowled. "Like never again?"

"Look at it this way. The attributes that made you friends won't disappear. They're like magnets that will attract you back again. If not, then the friendship wasn't that strong to begin with."

"I think that's some kind of new-age psychobabble stuff."

"Trust me, true friends will stick with you. You'll have your spats, but the good times will outweigh the bad."

At home, Cori went off to her room to study and go online. Hope was fully aware that her daughter spent hours each day with online friends. That was fine, as long as it didn't interfere with schoolwork or her chores. Priorities had to be set. Cori was smart enough to remember.

Hope sat down in front of her computer, and the screensaver was on. Max hadn't logged off.

"Good afternoon, Mrs. Herring."

Hope turned, and her immediate response was a laugh. "Oh my," she said. "Max, you have been busy."

# 13

---

"Do you like it?" Max asked, turning around, so Hope could get a good look at his black jumpsuit and thick boots.

"You look like some sort of mercenary," she said. "Straight out of a movie."

"Oh yes, moving pictures. I must admit that the ones I see on the computer are much more sophisticated than the ones I saw in the theaters while I was alive."

"Films have come a long way since then. In fact, most are no longer film at all. They're digital movies that occupy hard drives around the world."

"Yes, I realize that, although I'm not entirely clear on how a movie can be reduced to a great number of zeroes and ones."

"Not everyone understands binary, and I certainly don't have anything more than the tiniest idea of how computers work. In any case, it would seem that almost everything can be reduced to numbers, and numbers can be reduced to ones and zeroes. It's all a black box, as far as I'm concerned."

"I understand your reference. In my day, we had charlatans who claimed to have invented perpetual motion machines. Scientists told us that such machines were impossible, but scalawags and conmen would roll through the state, displaying their contraptions and begging for investors. The machines were invariably fake. I remember one such wooden box that was powered by a very small man, cleverly hidden inside. Of course, the ruse was eventually outed, but not before some poor souls had been bamboozled out of their money."

"When something is too good to be true…"

"Then it's too good to be true," Max finished. "So, Mrs. Herring, what is the word on the recent death?"

"Well, it's no longer a suicide."

"She didn't die of exhaust poisoning?"

"Oh, she did, but she was knocked unconscious before she was placed in the car. Someone killed her."

"That is something altogether different, isn't it. I

suspect you will have your hands full solving this one."

"I'm not so sure. I'm a suspect because I'm the one who found her in the car."

"That's right. Well, if I were a detective, I would cross you off my list immediately. You are far too fine a person to commit such a heinous crime."

"Thank you for saying so, but fine people commit murder, too. I don't think I'm at the top of the list, but I think I'm still on it."

"A travesty, if you ask me. In any case, you must now solve the murder to make sure no one will ever suspect you. I shall help where I can."

"Thank you very much. Your aid is always appreciated."

"I'm afraid, Mrs. Herring, that I have not been dedicated to researching your husband's case and his possible murderer. I have had far too much fun looking at moving pictures and examining new clothes. Forgive me for my lack of seriousness."

"Nothing to forgive. You gave over a century to your quest to find your own killer. You need a break. Having a bit of fun will simply rejuvenate you."

"Indeed. I will leave you to your work then. Halloween is tomorrow night, isn't it?"

"It is."

"Then, I will be on alert. There will be no shenanigans on my watch." Max stood up straight.

"Your attention will be appreciated."

Max saluted and faded away, leaving Hope amused. Max was transforming right before her eyes. He was becoming happier and more at ease. He was less stiff and serious which made him even more personable and likable.

After dinner, Hope once again settled into her office chair and worked on her lesson plans for the next day. She had scarcely begun, when Cori called from downstairs.

"Mom, someone's here to see you."

"Coming," Hope called and looked at her watch. *Who would come visiting at this hour?*

Hope found Elizabeth Scott waiting by the front door.

"Elizabeth," Hope said. "Come in and sit down. Coffee?"

"No, no, I can't stay. I just wanted to talk for a few minutes."

"About school?"

"In a way."

The assistant principal was the opposite of Ardis Warren. Elizabeth was tall and thick and strong looking. Her medium length, brown hair was cut in a blunt bob. Her face was pale, her eyes a light blue. Hope wasn't sure she knew exactly how many children Elizabeth had, but it was more than two or three. She looked older than she was.

"Actually," Elizabeth said, "it's about Ardis."

"What about Ardis?" Hope wondered what secret Elizabeth might want to reveal.

"You're well known for solving murders, and right now, I'm on the hook for Ardis's murder. The police are going to question me, because there was some bad blood between Ardis and me."

"Bad blood? What was wrong?"

"I was pretty vocal when Ardis was chosen to be principal over me. By all accounts, I was next in line for the position when Wanda Basset, the former principal, took the administrator job at the central office. The school board brought in Ardis from one of the other district schools. I got passed over, and I was furious. Frankly, I needed the raise being in the principal position would have given me. I still need the money. I know you have a child, Hope."

Hope nodded.

"Well, multiply your cost for one child by five and you'll come close to how expensive it is for me. In fact, mine cost more since one of my sons is autistic. His needs are through the roof. I would share, but you have no desire or need to know. I get that. Most people don't want to know my troubles. I don't even want to know my troubles. How sad is that?"

"What happened between you and Ardis?" Hope prompted.

"Oh, yes, well, like I said, I was vocal, and I said some things I shouldn't have. I thought I got a raw deal. I wanted that known."

Hope studied the woman's face. "Did you threaten Ardis?"

"No, no, never an actual threat. I did say that I wouldn't cry if something happened to her. Yeah, I said that. But I never said I was going to do something to her."

"Are there people who will remember your non-threat?"

"Look, I played sports all through high school and college, and I'm aggressive. It's my nature. I also get ahead of myself at times, saying things I don't actually mean. Athletes are always going to 'kill' the other girl. It's a mindset, not an actual thing."

Hope could see that Elizabeth was not one who would use deceit or bluffing to get what she wanted. Being bigger and stronger, she probably imposed her will on her opponent. If she were going to kill someone, she would probably just grab a gun and shoot.

"So, you're worried that your plain talk will get you in trouble. How does that involve me?" Hope asked.

"I want you to know that I didn't kill Ardis. In fact, I no longer wanted anything to happen to her. Since Ardis became principal, I've had an incredibly accommodating schedule. My kids' needs have been met, and I've managed to keep my job...all because of Ardis. If she had wanted, she could have made my life a living hell. So, I had no reason to kill her."

"You're the acting principal. Do you expect it to become permanent?"

"I don't know, and right now, I don't care. Oh, I want the job, but I'm not going to be upset if I don't get it. I would rather have someone like Ardis in the head office, someone who will allow me to come and go on a flexible basis."

"Elizabeth, I believe you," Hope said. "But, you have to remember I'm a suspect, too."

"You? When did you ever threaten Ardis? She adored you."

"Her feelings don't mean a thing. I'm the one who found Ardis, so the police will naturally investigate me."

"I suppose that's right, but they won't find anything. No offense, Hope, but you're far too nice to have whacked Ardis. And, I think you're far too smart. If you committed the murder, it wouldn't look like a murder at all."

"You give me too much credit."

Hope talked to Elizabeth for another ten minutes, listening to her describe a life with five children and a husband, a life that left little time for anything she'd dreamed of doing.

"So, tell me," Hope said, "who do you think might have killed Ardis?"

Elizabeth didn't hesitate. "For my money, it was someone in the family. Her husband or her son. They're both pretty worthless, if you ask me."

"Oh? How so?"

"Jim Warren is a womanizer. He has been since high school. I don't know how Ardis put up with him for all these years. I suppose she got used to it. I know that Ardis has had words with more than one woman in Castle Park. I'm no gossip, so you should ask Jim yourself. If he says he stopped chasing skirts long ago, he's lying."

"And her son?"

"Jim Jr. is a money pit. He's been chasing his dream of becoming a golf professional for years. Oh, don't get me wrong, he's good. He's just not good enough. Mostly, because he doesn't practice enough. He lacks the grit a great athlete needs. Trust me, I know. I've been around pro athletes all my life. They have a focus amateurs don't have."

"Ardis supported her son?"

"How many golf schools can someone attend? How many years can someone spend on the junior-junior-junior tour? He was sucking Ardis dry. At least, that's how I saw it."

"That's a shame."

Five minutes later, Elizabeth was gone. Hope locked the door and found Cori standing behind her.

"Did you hear all that?" Hope asked.

Cori shook her head. "Only the last part. She came here to tell you about Mr. Warren and his son?"

"No, she came to tell me that she's innocent. She wanted to make sure that I knew that before I started helping the police."

"But, you're not helping because you're a suspect, right?"

"Correct. Now, it's almost time for bed."

"Yeah. I'm tired."

"Halloween tomorrow. Trick or treat."

Cori smiled. "I know. It will be great."

"Free candy always is."

In bed, Hope tried to push Elizabeth Scott's visit into the background. She'd spent enough time that day thinking about Ardis's murder.

But a different concern popped into her head. Lottie. Whether Cori knew it or not, her best friend was an influence on her. If the teen turned toward trouble, Cori would be affected.

As she pulled up her quilt, Hope sighed and closed her eyes.

## 14

While the death of Ardis Warren was still news, it slipped to the background for Hope and her students. Halloween had arrived, and that meant the class was consumed with costumes and candy and tricks—if there weren't treats. She didn't mind letting them chat before class, but, once the bell rang, they had to put all the excitement away. School was school. Her students understood that.

Even Cori was excited, talking about her costume and all the candy she was going to "score." Hope half wondered if she had enough candy in the house for all the trick-or-treaters that might knock on her door.

"We have plenty," Cori said. "You have to

remember that half the kids think our house is haunted. They're scared of it so they'll stay away."

"They're still afraid of it? We've lived here for a while now. Aren't they over the 'haunted' thing?"

"You'd be surprised." Cori grinned. "There are kids who think there's a ghost in the house. I guess they're not wrong."

"There could be two ghosts in the house. Maybe I'm one of them. I'm scary." Hope laughed, and Cori rolled her eyes.

"You're scary because you're a teacher, not because we have a ghost in the attic."

Hope pretended she was shocked. "You think there's a ghost in the attic?"

"Yup. I've met him. Some of the kids think they see someone moving around in the attic, and they yell 'ghost.'"

"Well, they do see someone moving around in the attic. It's me. My office is up there. Max wouldn't allow people outside the house to see him. Haven't you told them I work up there?"

"A thousand times. Some kids really aren't very smart."

"I'm sure it's just a case of wanting to believe in spirits. They want to believe there are ghosts and witches and vampires and whatnot. It adds color and drama to their lives. Like Lottie. Is she still changing as soon as she gets to school?"

"Oh, yeah. Turns out, she has this girl she talks to online. It's weird."

"You know this online girl?"

"No."

"Can you find out?"

"Probably."

"If that girl is influencing Lottie, you and her parents should know."

"Why? You think it's someone bad?"

"The web is filled with people who don't have our best interests at heart."

Cori shrugged. "Like you haven't told me that before."

"It's true, and you know it. If you can, find out who Lottie is talking to."

"And then?"

"Then, we find out about this girl."

"That's prying."

"That's being a good friend. You two do look out for each other, don't you?"

"Yeah."

"Enough said."

"Roger that."

Max was waiting when Hope entered her office.

He still wore the black jumpsuit and boots, and he had added a black beret. He looked like the modern version of a French Foreign Legionnaire.

"Nice beret," Hope said.

"Thank you. I saw it, and well, I find it jaunty, don't you think?"

"Very jaunty. How are things going?"

"I must confess, I am not making any progress on the case at hand. Have you ever experienced the hotspots inside some of the things you read? I mean, I click on them because they often provide additional information on a topic. Well, the additional information is filled with more hotspots that lead to yet more places, and pretty soon I'm lost in a maze of my own creation. I find I can spend hours just jumping about, reading a bit here and a bit there."

"The greatest time waster in the history of the universe," Hope said. "People spend hours and days jumping about like a flea in a frying pan. They learn about a great many topics, but the learning is shallow. They're always off on some wild goose hunt. It's hard not to get caught up in it."

"How do you avoid that? There are so many interesting places to visit."

"Will power, I suppose. If you can't maintain

your focus, you drift aimlessly, a ship without a rudder."

"I understand that. You should go downstairs."

"Why? It's too early for any trick-or-treaters."

"Someone is coming to the door, someone I don't recognize."

"Good enough. Stay close?"

"Always."

When the knock came, Hope wasn't far away from the door. She put on her smile and opened it to find a man smiling back.

"Hope Herring?" he asked.

"That's me. If you're selling something, I'll tell you right now that you're wasting your time."

"I'm not, and I'm not trying to hit you up for candy. My name is Jim Warren. My mother is ... *was* Ardis Warren. Got a minute?"

Hope knew she could not say no to the young man so she opened the door wide. "Come in."

The man who passed her was tall and lean and blond. He looked like the golf professional he was. He wasn't wearing black. But then, lots of people didn't believe in mourning clothes anymore.

"Can I get you some coffee or something?" Hope asked.

"No, thanks, I don't have a lot of time. I ... well, I

came for two reasons. One, I'd like to hear how you found my mother. And two, two is about you. I know you're the resident Sherlock Holmes. I want to know if you consider me a suspect."

"I see. Well, I'll tell you how I happened to be in the parking lot and how I went to your mother's car. I don't know much."

Hope went over the night of the gala and her discovery of the running car, the hose, and the efforts to save Ardis. Jim stood still, listening, which was a good trait. She supposed he learned his good manners from his mother. A school teacher doesn't become something else when she goes home.

"You didn't see anyone else out there, right?" he asked.

"No one. But then, I wasn't looking, and it was dark."

"Exactly. Now, on to part number two. Am I a suspect?"

"Should you be?"

"I suppose I can't avoid it. I believe it's common knowledge that I have yet to make it as a golf professional. I'm close, very close, but there are a million guys who are almost good enough. The world is full of them. And, chasing that dream is expensive.

Travel and lessons and entry fees and whatever, it's no country for the poor."

"I suppose your parents were helping out."

"My mother was. She was the one with the money, and I can't lie. She believed in the dream almost as much as I did. She fronted me."

"That changed?"

"You're too smart for me to lie to, so, yes, she had decided that it was time to pass on joining the tour and get a real job. She wanted me to find a wife and a house and a career that didn't depend on sinking a ten-foot putt under pressure. She told me there comes a time when we have to put aside sports and go to work."

"You're not ready for that?"

"No, I'm not. I'm still young, and I'm good. I suppose every golfer thinks that. But good isn't great, and you have to be great to make it. If I weren't so close, it would be easier. Do you understand that? If you're only five feet, ten inches tall and slow, you're not looking to make it in the NBA. Being *almost* there is cruel."

"Did your mother have a will, and do you know the contents?"

He smiled, and his pale blue eyes weren't teary.

"That's the reality of the situation, isn't it? Did I

have a motive for killing my mother? I suppose I did. She had a will, and she left me a chunk of change. Not enough to live comfortably for the rest of my life, but enough to keep my dream alive. So, I suppose you have to consider me a suspect. I'll tell you right now, I did not kill her. I ... couldn't. I loved her. Like most sons, I didn't tell her that often enough, but it's true."

"I believe you. Where were you when she died?"

"You know I was there, right?"

"The Mad Hatter."

"Yes. Alice in Wonderland was one of my favorite books growing up. I used to look for a rabbit hole to fall into. Never found it, but not for lack of trying."

"And when your mother was killed? Where were you during that time?"

"Outside, in the parking lot. I had applied for a spot in the next tournament, and I was hoping to get a sponsor's exemption. They do that in pro tournaments. I was checking my email."

"Did you get in?"

"No, I didn't. That happens more often than not. There are only so many exemptions to go around."

"Don't they have Monday qualifying for golf pros?"

"Yes, they do, but I didn't have the money to go there and compete."

"You were hoping your mother would come up with the funds?"

"A horse goes to the same water hole until the water is gone."

Hope didn't quite know what to think of Jim Jr. He wasn't easy to read, which would have been a good thing for a golf professional. Getting too emotional wouldn't help on the course.

"No one saw you making the call?"

He shook his head.

"So, you don't have an alibi?"

"No, I don't. I know that looks bad, but it's the truth. You believe me?"

"I believe everyone," Hope answered, "until it's time not to believe."

"I promise, I didn't kill my mother. I never would."

"Fair enough. I hate to ask, but what about your father?"

"My father?"

"I've heard rumors about him, and I was wondering if he might have a motive."

Jim rubbed his face and bit his lip, clearly not comfortable with Hope's question.

"I tried to stay away from my parents' problems. I have enough of my own. So, I'll tell you this much. I know my dad was not always faithful to my mom. He might lie about that, but it's the truth. Was it bad enough for them to get a divorce or something? I don't know."

"You said your mother had the money. Your father didn't?"

"No, my dad calls himself an entrepreneur, which is sometimes a fancy word for being without a steady job. I suppose I take after him. My mother was the worker, and she inherited some money from her worker parents."

Hope would have liked to push Jim harder, especially about his father, but she sensed that the son was not comfortable with that line of inquiry.

"I suppose I should get going," Jim said. "I know how this looks. But, I want to find my mother's killer. I'll help in any way I can."

"Just tell the truth," Hope said. "Lying only makes you look guilty."

"I'll remember that."

After he left, Cori appeared.

"That's the principal's son?" Cori asked.

"It is."

"Did he do it?"

"I don't know. He's a suspect, but then so am I."

"You don't have a reason to off the principal. Does he?"

"He'll inherit a 'chunk of change.' Those were his words."

"That's a reason. Why do people kill for money?"

"Good question, but it's not just for money. People kill for revenge and envy and hatred and love."

"People don't kill for love."

"They think they do. Sometimes, they can't stand the thought of someone else having what they want."

"That's the same as money," Cori stated. "You have it, they don't, so they kill for it."

"It is, in a way. Ready for trick-or-treat?"

"Changing the subject?"

"Murder isn't a topic for the dinner table."

"We're not at dinner," Cori said. "And, yes, I'm ready."

"Lottie is coming here for you?"

"Yep. And, don't be surprised if she sort of changes her costume while she's here."

"Cori!"

"Not much, not a lot, well, a lot, but if she didn't do it here, she'd do it outside behind a bush or something. You wouldn't want that to happen, would you?"

Hope rolled her eyes. It was just like Cori to choose the lesser of two evils.

"I would like it if Lottie didn't change her costume in the first place."

Cori shrugged. "So would I, so I had to pick door number two."

"All right, I'll accept that ...for the moment. I'll depend on you to take a good look at her costume and tell her if it's too ... just too."

"She won't listen to me, Mom."

"Yes, she will, because you'll threaten to have me intervene. She knows that if I have to pass judgment, her mother will soon know."

"Leverage, you always have leverage," Cori sighed. "Oh, by the way, the girl Lottie has become chummy with online is named Exotic Kitty."

"You're kidding."

Cori headed for her room. "Nope. Exotic Kitty on Instagram."

Hope stared after her daughter. What girl ever named herself "Exotic Kitty"?

## 15

Hope opened the door, and Lottie marched in.

"Hello, Lottie, ready for some candy?"

"You bet, Mrs. Herring. Is Cori in her room?"

"Sure, you know the way."

"Roger that."

Hope wanted to laugh. It seemed all the kids in Cori's class had picked up the lingo.

As Lottie passed, Hope took a careful look at the vampire. There was nothing risqué about her costume. It was the usual mix of red and black, fangs, dress, and long cape. If Cori expected her mother to raise some kind of protest, she was sadly mistaken. Hope didn't see any reason to do anything.

While she still meant to counsel Lottie, especially about her manner of dress, Hope wasn't about to spoil a fun evening for the teens. They would have to grow up soon enough.

While she waited for the girls to emerge from Cori's room, Hope set up her table of candy. She didn't expect a lot of traffic, as her house had been the proverbial "haunted house." She knew a lot of children would remember the fear and not knock on the door, even though they knew the house was under new ownership. She didn't blame them. It took years for the house to become a place of fear. It would take years for that fear to dissipate. She didn't mind. She didn't need a lot of kids coming by. It was one of the reasons she didn't go all out with decorations. Other families did, and that was good, but Hope simply handed out the candy.

She also had the protection of Max, who was more than capable enough to stop any child from performing a "trick." He didn't sleep, not really, so he was awake at all hours. And, he could make even the bravest boy turn tail and run like the dickens. He was her built-in alarm system.

In a way, she wished he could accompany Cori as she walked about the neighborhood. An invisible bodyguard would be a real asset. No one would dare mess with anyone Max was protecting. But, she knew that although he did wander outside of the house at night, he was wary about it and didn't travel far, lest he be scooped up by some sort of ghost vacuuming system. She didn't understand the mechanics, and she wasn't sure he did. She couldn't ask him to risk his existence. That would be too much.

The girl who came out of Cori's room was not the same Lottie who walked in. Hope was ... stunned.

The black dress had been raised way above Lottie's knees. It was so short that Hope didn't think Lottie could sit without revealing far more than anyone should. Her top had become blood stained to the extreme, with a V-neck that was designed for a much more mature female. Lottie's makeup was straight out of some horror show—black eyes and lips, skin so pale to the point of being white, a trickle of blood running down her chin. She was like no vampire Hope had ever seen.

"We'll be back," Lottie called as she hurried past, before Hope could comment.

Hope minded, but she didn't mind enough to grab the girl and start a lecture. Instead, she blocked Cori before she could slip past.

"I warned you," Cori said before Hope could say a word.

"I know you did. And, it was a fair warning. I'd

like to think I wasn't too stunned to say something to her, but that's not true. She surprised me."

"She does that a lot."

"All right then, I won't keep you. I'll tell you what, though. Later on tonight, I want you to take a picture of her and send it to me."

"Mom."

"I mean it. I will send it to Lottie's mother, with the proviso that she cannot tell Lottie where the picture came from. In fact, Lottie's mom shouldn't even bring it up. It's not necessary. Lottie shouldn't be punished for what she's done. Her mother simply needs to provide more supervision. Got it?"

"She'll know it's me."

"Maybe. Doesn't matter. If she asks, tell her the truth ... then lie."

"What?" Confusion washed over the teen's face.

"Admit you took the pic, but say I was the one who found it and passed it along, which is mostly true. Got it?"

"Got it."

"You want your friend to get ahead of whatever is pushing her. You take the pic. I'll do the rest."

Cori tugged her witch's hat down on her head. "You know, I could use a good spell right now, one that would turn Lottie back into who she used to be."

"Be careful what you wish for." Hope hugged her daughter. "You look terrific. Have a good time. Go scare some people."

"I can do that even without a costume."

"Hah! Go."

Hope watched Cori disappear, just as a group of elves and fairies ran up the drive. Hope guessed they were all under eight, and they laughed as they came to the door. Most of them carried orange, plastic pumpkins that already had a few candy bars in them. Hope couldn't help but smile.

"Trick or treat!"

Their voices were filled with joy and anticipation. Hope cooed over them and chatted as she passed out the candy. They were polite, adding a "thank you" for every piece of chocolate. They ran off, giggling like the elves and fairies they were. She watched as they passed three pirates with eyepatches and swords. The night had begun. Darkness was just around the corner. Hope could expect a steady stream of costumes and polite responses to her questions. The night was warm and clear. Parents wouldn't have to deal with water-soaked costumes and water-logged candy.

After an hour and a half, Hope thought about Lottie and Cori. She knew they would be coming back in a little while. She also knew there would be a photo on her phone. She'd have to find a way to get it to Lottie's mother, without creating too wide a trail. Lottie wasn't dumb. She might remember the photo and who took it. That would strain the relationship ... it might even end it. Hope didn't want that. Good friends were hard to find.

Lottie and Cori returned as the Halloween river became a stream that would soon be a trickle. Hope stayed by the door, ready to greet the stragglers. She had a good idea what was happening in Cori's bedroom, and she wasn't wrong.

Within minutes, the teens came out, and Lottie had gone through a reverse transformation. The dress hung past her knees, her top was modest to the extreme, if a little bloody. She said a quick good-bye to Hope, with Cori following behind. They had agreed they would walk together half way and then split off. That way neither one had to walk all the way home alone. Hope was comfortable with that. Without some risk, life contained little flavor.

When Cori returned, Hope turned off the porch light. Halloween was officially over. She retreated to the kitchen, where Cori was pouring herself a glass of lemonade.

"Thirsty work?"

"You would not believe it. Why do some people think an apple is better than a candy bar? I mean, please, it's Halloween."

"They're thinking of your teeth, perhaps."

"Not a chance. They're virtue signaling," Cori said.

"Virtue signaling?"

"You know what I mean. Giving out apples doesn't do anything for the trick-or-treaters," Cori told her mother. "It's all about the people handing out the apples. They want to feel good about themselves and send a message to everyone else. Hey, look at me, I'm giving out healthy stuff. I'm helping everyone get their fruit ration for the day."

"My, my, such cynicism from one so young. You don't think those people are for real?"

"Mom, it's not cynicism. It's truth. You see it every day at school. Everyone drives up in an SUV that has a SAVE THE PLANET bumper sticker, or something like that."

"You notice those things?"

"You taught me to notice lots of things."

"Like Lottie?"

"I told you what she would do. I warned you she'd change clothes."

"Yes, you did. Still, I was a little overwhelmed by what she did. Is that the worst she's ever looked?"

"Almost. She was pretty sure she could get away with more because it's Halloween. People cut us more slack when it's a costume."

"Agreed. Did you get a picture or two?"

"I did, and I tried to do it when she wasn't looking. Can you believe that dress? It hardly covered her butt."

"I noticed. And the top wasn't made for someone her age."

"I tried to tell her that, but she doesn't care. She says Exotic Kitty loves a top like that."

"Exotic Kitty. I was meaning to ask you about that. It's a girl?"

"Yeah, older than us, but not by much. She has an Instagram presence."

"Presence?"

"Lots of people following her account. She does these videos, and trust me, she wears the same stuff Lottie does, only worse."

"Should I take a look at her stuff?"

"Not unless you have to. It embarrasses me sometimes."

"Does Lottie communicate directly with Exotic Kitty?"

"Oh yeah, Lottie is one of the Kitty-Kats, part of the inner circle. I don't know how many are on that level, but Lottie is one of them. She gets a lot of email and texts that others don't get."

"And, Lottie sends stuff to Kitty?"

"Absolutely. She sends pics of her at school. Kitty goes wild."

"Does Kitty tell Lottie to keep their relationship quiet?"

"Yeah. Lottie says her parents would never understand what's happening all around us. People like Kitty and Lottie are going to be famous, and famous people make a lot of money."

"It's about money?"

"Pretty much. People with a presence get paid for the traffic. I'm not sure how it all works, but it works."

"Has Lottie started posing on Instagram?"

Cori turned away, and Hope knew what that meant.

"Cori?"

"Yeah, she has. She doesn't have many followers, but she has some. Exotic Kitty is helping her."

"Have you seen Lottie's videos?"

Cori shook her head. "I don't want to see that stuff."

"You might take a peek."

"Why would I do that?"

"So, you'll know what you're missing."

"Missing?"

"We all wonder about things that other people find worthwhile. We wonder what all the hype is about. In some cases, we're missing out on a good thing. That happens. More often, we're missing out on what we should miss out on. Does that make sense?"

"No."

Hope laughed. "It's true, though. So, don't be afraid to examine something, even if you think you won't like it. You never know."

"Like trying Brussel sprouts?"

"Exactly."

"I didn't think I'd like them, and I don't."

"Just keep trying new stuff."

"And, if I tumble into some kind of weird funk?"

"I'll lock you in your room without a phone or computer...for weeks."

"I won't last that long. I'm going to bed."

"Yep, tomorrow is a school day. Don't stay up too long."

"I won't."

Hope kissed Cori and watched her head off to bed. It was still too early for Hope to sleep, so she headed up to the attic office. She found Max, in his jaunty beret, sitting at the computer. He turned as she entered.

"Good evening, Mrs. Herring. Did you know you can find out how to do absolutely anything on a site named YouTube?"

"And, what did you find out how to do?"

"Make the computer absolutely quiet. The speakers, that's right, isn't it?"

Hope nodded.

"The speakers are off, and I learned how to make the keyboard as quiet as the mouse."

"You're amazing."

"No, I'm really wasting time, aren't I?"

"No, you've made it so you won't be heard when you're online, and that's a good thing."

Max smiled. "I'm glad you approve. I suppose you want to use your computer now."

"I need to check my email."

"May I ask a favor? Would it be all right if I establish my own email account? I have found some rather interesting historians that I might wish to correspond with, and I would feel ill at ease if I used your account."

"Of course, I should have thought of that myself. Do you need help?"

"Not one iota. I have always believed that people learn best by doing. And, I have all those experts on the computer who will show me how to do it."

"Exactly. If you need help…"

"I shall immediately ask. Good night, Mrs. Herring."

"Good night, Max."

Hope watched as Max disappeared. Then, she settled in her chair, surprised that she didn't find it warm. But then, Max was a ghost. He didn't generate heat … he didn't have to.

Most of her email was the vanilla type she received every day. Yet, there was one that surprised and intrigued her. It was from Jim Warren Sr, and it asked if he could talk to her after school the next day. Hope was a little surprised, but she welcomed the opportunity to talk to a fellow suspect.

"Certainly." Hope replied.

# 16

Hope was correcting homework at her desk, when Jim Warren Sr. walked into the room. What struck Hope immediately was the air of confidence the man exhibited. He wore a dark gray suit with a narrow pinstripe, blue shirt, and black tie which she assumed indicated that he was in mourning. His blond hair wasn't as thick as his son's, but it was styled and swept back. She guessed he used a generous amount of hair product. He wasn't heavy, but he wasn't thin either. He looked comfortable with himself, smiling a handsome smile. She knew he would attract women, no matter what he did. He was that sort of man.

"Hope. May I call you Hope?" He possessed a nice voice too, not too high-pitched or whiny.

"Sure," Hope replied.

"Call me Jim or Jimmy. Doesn't matter. I answer to almost anything. That's not a problem ... generally."

She stood and shook his hand. He had a firm grip, which she appreciated.

"I've heard a great deal about you," he said. "You are by far the best detective in this county and state. There is no doubt about that. The fact that you're attractive probably makes the job easier."

Hope noticed the immediate step into mild flirting. His blue eyes seemed to twinkle, as if he were playing some sort of game.

"It's more like a hobby. I don't get paid or anything."

"Then, perhaps, I can change that. How would you like to work as a detective ... for me?"

"I'm afraid I'm not qualified. No license, no office, no way to charge you."

"We can work something out, I'm sure."

His smile said he was genuinely flirting, and she wasn't all that impressed. Yet, she returned the smile, hoping it would make him a bit reckless.

"I'm sure," she said. "But the police are already working the case. I would be redundant."

"The police are near-sighted, as far as I'm

concerned. They're still thinking I might have done something to Ardis."

"Did you?" Hope tilted her head to the side in question.

"No, of course, not. I'm not a violent man. I don't need fists to get what I want. Besides, I loved my wife and she loved me, no matter what other people might say."

"I'm sure she did. But, you did have some problems, didn't you?"

"Problems? I suppose so, but those came about because of senseless gossip and envy. Believe me, Hope, there are people in this town who would love to see me fall flat on my face. Success breeds enemies. That's as clear as the day is long."

"So, do you think one of your enemies killed Ardis?"

"I wouldn't be surprised. People go to great lengths to harm their betters. It's as simple as Cain and Abel. Cain couldn't take the heat, so he killed his brother. Being second best wears on some people."

"Who would qualify as a suspect?"

"I don't have a name for you, not right now. I will, however, put my brain to work and come up with some people who bear investigating."

"Have you offered those names to the police?"

"Not yet. Frankly, I hadn't given that angle all that much thought. You put that excellent idea in my head. No wonder everyone in Castle Park admires you."

Hope smiled, recognizing the way he patronized her. She also knew that some women would eat up the praise. Everyone liked to be told how wonderful they were.

"Before we get into that," Hope said. "Where were you when Ardis was attacked?"

"I had stepped into Ardis's office to make a call. I have business contacts all around the world, and because of time zones, I frequently make calls at night. You understand."

"Why the office?"

"Privacy. When you're negotiating lucrative business deals, you need to play your cards close to the vest. I didn't wish to be overheard. Everyone else was at the gala. It was perfect."

*Since everyone was at the gala*, Hope thought, *it would be perfect for any sort of tryst that required privacy.*

"You were alone then?"

"I was. And, I don't think anyone saw me enter or

leave the office. I don't recall running into anyone in the hall."

"I see. You must realize that without an alibi, you're a suspect. Did you give the police your phone, so they could validate the call?"

"That's the problem, Hope. I lost my phone. I have no idea what happened to it. I was in a sort of funk after I heard about Ardis. I must have left it some place."

"The locator app can't find it?"

"No. It must be off or something."

"No matter. The police can get a copy of your phone bill and find the call."

"Yes, I suppose they can. Will they do that?"

"They'll need to verify your alibi."

He nodded, and Hope could tell that he hadn't thought about the record the phone service would provide. That led her to believe that maybe the telephone call had never happened.

"I'm sure they will." His smile returned. "I should tell you that I would bet that Ardis's sister is the murderer."

"Oh, why?"

"Well, for one thing, there is a generous bequest to her in Ardis's will and Abby needs the money. She has never been able to make ends meet. Ardis provided some support, but, recently, she decided that she was merely enabling her sister's bad behavior. So, she cut her off."

"That must have been traumatic for both women."

"It was, especially for Abby. She works as some sort of virtual travel agent. You know, from her home, and she gets paid a pittance. You know what happens to people who work at home." He filled his cheeks with air, showing the effects of sitting and eating for hours at a time. "So, she's not exactly marrying material. No man of any intelligence will go near her."

Hope wondered why he was so critical of his sister-in-law. Hope guessed there was some bad blood between Jim Sr. and Abby.

"Was Abby at the gala?" Hope asked.

"I don't know. I believe she was, but she wasn't in a costume or anything."

"Why would she be there then?"

"To beg for money. I think she might be getting kicked out of her apartment."

"Did you see her? Did anyone see her?"

"I didn't, but I think several people did notice her hanging around. I was busy helping Ardis run the gala."

"Right. The hose from the exhaust would indicate that the murderer came prepared to kill. You think Abby could plan like that?"

Jim frowned, and Hope could tell that he hadn't thought of the hose. Or, maybe he was just putting on an act.

"Abby is no brain trust, but she is bright enough to do some research and come up with the hose. I mean, she's on her computer all the time. If she wanted to learn how to murder someone, she could find it."

"Then, the police will probably do a forensic search on her computer. You have a computer too, don't you?"

Jim Sr. nodded and blinked several times, a sign that he hadn't yet cleaned his computer of incriminating information.

"I don't think they even need Abby's computer," Hope continued. "They can probably simply use the IP address or something."

"That makes sense. Now, I know why people think you're so clever, Hope. You think of everything."

"Hardly. All right, Abby had a reason to commit murder. Who else?"

"Who else?"

"If you're going to hire me, then I have to know who else you think was capable of murder."

"Hire you? Oh, yes, that would be wonderful. I tell you what, Hope. I need a little bit of time to put together my list of likely suspects. You can understand that, right? I came here to tell you about being in the office when Ardis died. So, that task was accomplished. I wasn't prepared to brief you on the other ... stuff."

"Quite all right, Jimmy. When you're ready, call or email. We'll arrange something."

He grinned at the thought of "arranging" something. Hope could read his mind. He wasn't all that clever.

"Of course, and you can come to my house. I can show you everything."

He winked, and Hope smiled. She couldn't help but wonder if his little act worked on other women. She supposed it did, since he was rumored to be quite the ladies' man.

When she was sure he was gone, she called Detective Robinson and filled him in on her meeting with Jim Sr. If he was quick, he could probably get to Jim Sr.'s computer and telephone records before he had a chance to erase the trail. Detective Robinson was happy for the tip. He considered Jim Sr. to be a prime suspect, as was Jim Jr., since both would benefit from the death of Ardis. He had not yet interviewed Abby, but he would make a point of it.

Hope considered trying to talk to Abby before the police scared her to death, but then decided that wouldn't be a good idea, since Hope was also a suspect. The farther she stayed from the other suspects, the better.

Before Hope left for the day, she pulled out her phone and pulled up the pics Cori had sent the night before. Cori had a good eye, and the photos were revealing. The question was whether or not to send them to Lottie's mother. Hope wanted to be discreet about the pictures. She didn't want to initiate some kind of family problem. In all probability, Adele Wells knew about her daughter's dress code. Did Adele know about Exotic Kitty? That might come as a surprise to Adele, who probably granted Lottie some privacy. As far as Hope was concerned, Exotic Kitty was the greater danger. She didn't appear to be the sort of girl that Lottie should be emulating.

Hope tapped her phone.

Send or not send?

She was at that point where she needed to make a decision. She could try to help a young girl, or she could destroy her daughter's best friendship. And there was no guarantee that anything she did would make any difference.

Not trying sounded cowardly to Hope.

She wrote her message carefully, choosing words that might soften the blow. She didn't want to push Adele away. Then, she wondered if Adele would simply say "go to hell" and never speak to her again. That could happen. Some parents didn't appreciate honest criticism, and anyway, Hope wasn't trying to criticize. But it would come out that way. She couldn't help that.

With a sigh, Hope sent the note and pictures. It was time to grab Cori and head for home. She told herself that if things soured, she could always console herself with the chocolate candy that was left over from the night before. She wasn't a binge chocoholic, but she could imitate one.

Her phone pinged before Hope reached the door. She stopped and opened up the app. The note was a reply from Adele.

*We need to talk.*

She read the message and supposed that it meant bad news. Those four words signaled the death of more relationships than any other four words in the English language. Hope was tempted to reply, but she held off. If she answered too quickly, Adele would think events had reached crisis mode. That wasn't what Hope wanted at all. She wanted everyone to remain calm, so the problem could be sorted out and solved.

Her phone chirped, and she frowned. Had Adele followed up with a call? She looked at the caller ID —*PRIVATE*. Hope knew very few people who kept their ID private, and she was inclined to ignore the call. But something made her decide to answer.

"Hi, this is Hope," she said.

"Hello, this is Abby Harris. Ardis Warren was my sister. I would like to talk to you."

## 17

Hope picked up Cori and started for home. While she drove, she considered everyone who wanted to talk to her. There was Adele Wells, Lottie's mother, and Abby Harris, Ardis's sister. Hope also needed to talk to Jim Sr., who, no doubt, was planning some sort of tryst at his house. Men like Jim Sr. were easy to read. Hope's question was who to talk to first. She supposed Abby was the logical choice. The murder of Ardis was more important than Exotic Kitty. Lottie's problems would hold for a while. They weren't life or death.

"Why, my day was just fine," Cori said suddenly. "Thank you for asking. I aced my social studies quiz and was asked to try out for the school play. Not that I'm an actress or anything. But, I must admit I do well on stage. To be or not to be ... or something like that."

"Ha, ha," Hope said. "I get it. You feel neglected when you're not subjected to twenty questions."

"Well, most days, I don't have much information to pass along, but today is different. Here I am, chock full of news, and you don't even ask. What is a girl to do?"

"I'm all ears. Oh, wait, gee, Cori, what did you do today? Any fantastic news?"

"Snarky, Mom, snarky. Tell me what you know about a play titled *Our Town*. And don't tell me to look it up."

"Of course, look it up, but I'll tell you what I know. "*Our Town* is an award-winning play by Thornton Wilder. It's about a fictional town in New Hampshire. I forget the name. It covers the first decade of the twentieth century, I believe. Again, my memory doesn't serve me well sometimes. I would think the play is too old for a class your age. I mean, lots of adult roles."

"That's what our teacher said. Part of the challenge is adapting the play to our class. I get to try out for Emily Webb."

"If I remember correctly that was a good role."

"I think so. I have to read the play. You don't mind if I try out?"

"Of course, not. You have to keep trying new things."

"Because, you don't know what you're missing?" Cori smiled.

"Now, who's being snarky?"

Cori laughed. "Tis true."

At home, Hope took a quick hike up to her office where she found Max at the computer. He had changed into a tuxedo, black tie, white shirt, polished shoes. He looked like a wannabe Fred Astaire. He turned and smiled.

"Hello, Mrs. Herring. How was school?"

"You look quite dapper, Max. Going out?"

He laughed. "No, no, it's just been a hundred years since I wore a tuxedo. I ... well, back then, I did like dressing up once in a while. When I saw this online, I said why not? I may have no place to go, but I can still get gussied up, as we used to say."

"We should be a bit more formal sometimes. I do believe in that. Some rules make for polite society."

"Indeed, they do. Ah, I should vanish, as I am sure you have work to do."

"I do, and I don't. I want to check my email, and then, you can go back to using the computer."

"I don't know what's gotten into me. At times, I get so wound up with what I'm doing that I forget about your husband's pressing case. I mean, did you know that most of the paintings in the Louvre are online. You can delight in their beauty for hours."

"You never have to leave the house, Max, to take stock of the wonders of the world."

"I never would have known that if it hadn't been for you, Mrs. Herring."

Max faded to nothing, and Hope settled in the cold chair. She pulled up her mail and took care of anything pressing. Then, she called Abby Harris.

∽

Hope waved a hand in front of Cori, who sat at her desk, doing homework and listening to something on her earbuds.

"What?" Cori asked.

"I have to run out and talk to the principal's sister. You'll be all right here for an hour or so?"

"Sure. You know, this play is pretty good. I think I could do this."

"I'm sure you can. Confidence is the key to a lot of success … unless you really can't act."

"Right."

Hope kissed her daughter and headed for the car. She had already informed Max, so Cori would not be alone.

Abby's apartment was located in the poorer section of Castle Park. The parking lot was home to several cars on blocks and a reasonable amount of trash. She noted a number of teens hanging around on what had to have been a playground at one time. The swing frames were still in place, anchored in the concrete, but the swings and chains were long gone. The basketball court had one rim still in place. The other hung down at a ninety-degree angle. No one was playing. Careful to lock her car, Hope promised herself to make the visit short. She needed to be gone before dark.

Abby opened the door to the length of a chain and peered at Hope through the crack in the door.

"You the murder woman?"

"I help the police on occasion, but I wouldn't call myself the murder woman."

"One second."

Hope heard the person inside, removing the chain. The door opened.

"Come in. It's not healthy to talk out on the stoop."

Hope hurried inside and half wished she hadn't.

The first thing she noticed was the smell. The place smelled of old socks and cheap air freshener. She guessed the windows hadn't been opened in decades, and the carpet hadn't been cleaned in ... years. While it was a dark pattern, she could still make out stains and bald sections. It sure hadn't suffered from regular cleaning.

"Coffee?" Abby asked, after she had thrown five locks in place and attached the chain.

"No, I won't be staying long," Hope told her.

The second thing Hope noticed was the huge TV standing against one wall. She had to wonder about someone who would invest thousands in a TV and neglect normal maintenance. It said something about Abby's priorities, and it wasn't something good.

"That's good," Abby said. "People shouldn't hang around this place. I shouldn't be here either, but my job sucks. This is all I can afford."

Hope smiled and nodded. "Tell me, did you and Ardis get along?"

"Yes, considering we were sisters. She was older, and well, our parents doted on her. She was the smart one. I was just an add-on, if you know what I mean."

"I do. But, as I understand things, you're mentioned in her will."

"Who told you that? No, let me guess. You heard it from that blowhard Jim Senior. God, that guy couldn't keep his mouth shut in a sand storm. To answer your question, yes, I believe I will inherit something, perhaps something substantial. I need it. Trust me, if I live here another year, I'll be dead."

"I'll be honest with you. Jim Senior said Ardis supported you to some extent, and recently, she stopped the money."

"Mind if I smoke?"

Hope *did* mind, but she wasn't going to say so. It was Abby's place.

Abby didn't look younger than her sister. In fact, Abby looked older, heavier and more worn. She needed to lose forty pounds at least. Her hair was a mix of brown where she had dyed it, and gray where it had grown out of her scalp. Hope guessed that the dye wasn't necessary if Ardis was no longer footing the bill.

Abby's soft brown eyes were bloodshot. Hope had no idea what that meant. She watched as the woman lit a cigarette and moved to the battered couch.

"Yeah," Abby said. "My sister cut me off. Some

sister, huh? I mean, I can understand it, but she could have given me some warning. She could have weaned me off the money. That would have been thoughtful, but I can't say Ardis was ever thoughtful where I was concerned. You have a sister?"

"Yes," Hope said. "She lives in California. We don't see each other often."

"That's probably a good thing. All right, I might as well admit it. I had a reason to kill Ardis. I'm not going to get around that, no matter how hard I try. So, we'll go to question number two. Did I kill her? The answer is no. I would never do that. We might not have seen eye-to-eye all the time, but we were sisters. In our way, we loved each other. I don't care if you believe that, but it's true. She looked out for me, and I tried to help her when I could."

"How did you help her?"

"It was a couple months ago. She caught her husband cheating ... again. She wanted to divorce him, but she needed some time to set it up. You know how some wives are. They decide to dump their hubbies, and that starts a six-month process of draining the bank accounts."

"Ardis was putting away money?"

"Yep. She had me take the deposits to the bank, the one her husband didn't use. That way, she didn't have to worry about being spotted by him or any of his friends."

"That sounds like a lot of mistrust."

"Oh, it was probably worse than that. Old hubby had raided her savings account once, and she never forgot. Why she didn't divorce him back then, I have no idea. Ain't love grand?"

"All right, did she have an attorney?"

"No, not yet. Castle Park can be a hard place for a secret. She didn't want someone spotting her with some divorce attorney."

"That I understand. So, Ardis was working toward a divorce. You knew about it. Anyone else?"

"Not as far as I know, but I'm guessing someone else would know something. Hard not to."

"I agree. Next question. Were you at the gala the night Ardis died?"

Abby shook her head. "No, I'm not refined enough for one of those parties. I know my place."

"Were you at the school?"

Abby looked away and then looked back. "Did someone say I was?"

"Come on, Abby. If you were there, just say so, because the police will trace your cell phone, and if it pinged some tower near the school, they'll find out. And maybe, someone spotted you or your car. It doesn't help to lie."

"Yeah, I thought of that. Stupid phone. Can't go anywhere without it showing people where you've been. Sometimes, I think they're not worth what we pay for them."

"So, you were at the school?"

"I was. I wanted to talk to Ardis. I thought I could plead my case. You know, get her to agree to giving me some money for a month or two."

"Did you see her?"

"No. I missed her early, and once the place started hopping, I knew she wouldn't have time for me."

"Why did you come that particular night? I mean, you could have seen her during the day."

Abby laughed. "Darn it, you are good. The whole truth is I was at a bar, drinking. I got mad, and I decided I would just get in her face. You know how it is when you're half drunk. You do stupid things."

"Like put your sister in a car filled with carbon monoxide?"

"I didn't do that. I didn't even see her or talk to her. I got there, I heard the music and stuff, and I remembered it was the night of the big gala. I walked back to my car and drove home."

"Anyone see you?"

"Not after I left the Kit-Kat-Klub. Funny name, huh? The owner likes cats. Go figure."

Hope thought a moment. She didn't know whether or not to believe Abby. The woman sounded truthful, but most people sounded that way. The best liars always seemed like they were being honest. Hope had the feeling Abby was holding something back, but she didn't care. She didn't have the time nor energy to hang around.

"Here's what I'm going to do," Hope said. "Nothing."

"Nothing?" Abby looked surprised.

"Nothing, but you're going to go down to the police station and talk to Detective Robinson. You're going to tell him what you told me, all of it. I'll know if you don't talk to him, understand?"

She nodded.

"Do it tomorrow, first thing. I'll check with him later." Hope nodded at the door. "I'll be going now."

She watched as Abby opened all the locks and the chain.

"Do you believe me?" Abby asked softly.

"Yes and no. I don't think you killed your sister, but I do think you're holding something back. Leave it at that."

Hope hurried to her car and half raced away from the apartment complex. She checked her mirrors a lot, making sure no one followed. Fear could make people paranoid.

Cori and Bijou were waiting when Hope walked into the house. The cat rubbed against the woman's legs and Hope bent to pat her. "Hungry?" she asked her daughter. "I'll start dinner."

"No, you won't," Cori said. "We're invited to dinner at Lottie's house."

Hope's eyes widened. "We are?"

"And her mother says we can't say no."

# 18

Adele Wells greeted the Herring mother and daughter and immediately shunted Cori off to Lottie's bedroom. Cori didn't argue, and neither did Hope. Adele led Hope to the kitchen, where the chili was cooking on the stove.

"That smells delicious."

"I hope you like it," Adele said. "It's just the four of us tonight. Rob is away on a business trip."

Hope immediately noticed the fatigue in Adele's face. Perhaps, she hadn't been sleeping well, and Hope could probably guess why.

"I won't beat around the bush," Adele said. "The pictures you sent were disturbing. I'm sure you thought the same thing."

"I did," Hope said. "I don't want to interfere with

other families' personal stuff, but I thought you should know ... if you didn't already."

Adele's wan smile told Hope that Lottie's antics had not gone unnoticed.

"I knew, and I didn't know, if that makes sense. I mean, I knew she was changing at school, but I had no idea how far she had gone."

"Parents are rarely as dumb as their children think. We just don't see the need to fight over every little thing."

"Yeah, well, this thing may not be so little. Has Cori told you about Exotic Kitty?"

"She has, in broad terms. I'm not familiar with the whole Instagram thing."

"I'm not either, and I've held back doing a full investigation. I wanted Lottie to get over this on her own."

"We all hope our kids somehow manage to toss away bad habits. Doesn't happen all that often."

Adele poured two glasses of red wine and handed one to Hope.

"You're right. I'm rethinking my strategy. I may have to intervene. Before I do that, I wanted to get your opinion. Do you think this is just some phase she'll get over?"

Hope sipped her wine and thought a moment.

She wanted to help, but she knew she was no expert on child rearing.

"I'll tell you what I think," Hope said. "There are two ways to go about changing behavior. One is to nip the problem in the bud, before it becomes a full-blown weed. The other is to wait and see if the problem will take care of itself. You keep a close eye on what's happening, and you step in when you think the person has crossed the line."

"Which do you recommend?"

"There's no hard and fast rule. If you jump on her too early, you risk alienation. That will make her spiteful and rebellious. She'll keep doing what she's doing, only it won't be so easy to see."

"Like a drug addict or alcoholic? They become more clever about their vice?"

"Exactly."

"So, I should wait?"

"I didn't say that. Waiting breeds its own set of problems. Generally, these addictions don't jump out full blown. It's a steady, day-by-day accumulation of behaviors. It's like aging. You don't go from thirty to fifty overnight. The face in the mirror changes slowly. With addictions, by the time you notice the big change, it could be too late."

"What she's doing now is what she did yesterday,

but not what she did last week? I just can't compare the two?"

"Exactly. So, you're in trouble if you act early, and you're in trouble if you act late. I wish there was some sort of algorithm that would guarantee a good result, but we're dealing with unpredictable people. You just can't know."

Adele nodded and bit her lip. Hope understood the worry that consumed her friend.

"What would you do?" Adele asked.

"First, I will tell you that I'm glad I don't have to make this decision. Not, that I won't have to do something similar in the future. I probably will. As far as Lottie is concerned, I think I would do something now. You have a couple of things working in your favor. One, since she's hiding what she's doing, she knows it's wrong, or at least not acceptable. That's a good thing. When people get to the point where they don't hide stuff, then they believe that it's all right. That makes it harder to convince them otherwise."

"I get that. She still has a conscience."

"Exactly. How long till she thinks it's perfectly all right? I have no idea, but at some point, that might happen."

"Dear God, I wish I didn't have to think about this."

"The world is filled with temptations, and our daughters will have to do their best to stay away from them. You have to be strong enough to point out the downside of what they're doing. If they accept the negative behavior..." Hope shrugged.

"Go on," Adele said. "What else?"

"I believe that most of life is behavior. What you do means a great deal more than what you say. We're always working on instilling good behavior in children. Right now, Lottie has chosen what we think is bad behavior. So, that is what we're trying to change. We can't get inside her head and muck around. She's the only one who can control her thoughts."

"You think that will help?"

"Habits are very powerful. They take over and allow us to think. Good habits are beneficial. Bad habits? Well, we all have those, and we must work constantly to change them. So, I would start with Lottie's habits. The first would be Exotic Kitty. I think that is a real danger."

"If I forbid her to contact Exotic Kitty, she'll just sneak around me, right?"

"Wouldn't you?"

Adele nodded. "If I really wanted to, I'd still do it."

"Exactly. So, I doubt a ban would work. However, limits might. Lottie's contact can be time-bound. One hour a day, after dinner. And then, only if she's not changed clothes at school. She has to finish her homework, too. Those are reasonable conditions, and they can become habits. You might ask her to write down just why she likes this Exotic Kitty and why she needs to change her look at school. Having her examine her motives might reveal something to her. You can try substitution. Instead of Exotic Kitty, you might try sports or some other pastime."

"I get you. Keep her busy, but not too busy, and make sure she has a set of rules to follow."

"Yes. Make sure she knows that you know. She's not fooling anyone. If she wants to dress a bit on the wild side, tell her you'll agree ... to a point. You have to approve her clothes, and if she can't abide by that, you'll start taking away privileges."

"I would hate to punish her."

"Don't think of it that way. You're not punishing her, you're punishing the behavior. She can do pretty much what she wants, as long as it isn't unacceptable behavior. That's what earns the punishment."

"You make it sound so logical. Why is that?"

Hope shrugged. "I don't know. I'm not all that logical. To tell the truth, I just want to keep things simple. You do A, and B follows. Children like to make things complex. They invoke feelings and downplay behavior. I try not to subscribe to that. Behavior matters."

"You give good advice, Hope. I'll sit Lottie down and get started."

"You expect her to put up a fight?"

"I don't see why she wouldn't. She's been converted to this sort of thing. I mean, it's all over social media."

"It is, which makes it powerful. All the kids in school flock to the social media sites."

"Well, there's nothing I can do about all the kids, just Lottie. How about some food?"

"I'm all for it."

When the evening was over, Hope and Cori walked slowly down the sidewalks on their trip home. Hope wondered if Cori would want to know the outcome of the discussion in the kitchen.

"How much trouble is she in?" Cori asked.

"Not too much. I don't think Mrs. Wells is going to lock Lottie in the dungeon and feed her bread and water."

"Why not? I hear that's a real attitude adjustor."

Hope laughed. "So, I get to try it on you?"

"I didn't say that. My attitudes are already practically perfect. What did you and her decide?"

"I think I can safely say that things are going to change for Lottie. I don't know how much or how soon, but Lottie will have to adjust."

"No more Exotic Kitty?"

"Not *so much* Exotic Kitty. The first step to abstinence is control. They're going to try and wean Lottie off that particular addiction."

"It's not going to work."

"Why not?"

"Because Lottie no longer listens to her parents."

"She listens to Exotic Kitty?"

"Yep, and I'm pretty sure that Lottie will find ways to get around any sort of restraint."

"I would expect that, too. Then her parents will become even tougher."

"It will turn into a battle."

Hope thought a moment. "Do you think Lottie will blame you?"

"She's no dummy. We show up for dinner, and her mother says no more Kitty. Since you're pretty famous as a mystery solver, Lottie will know you put some thoughts into her mother's head."

"Don't tell her and don't deny it. Just say you

don't know. You didn't hear anything. That's the truth."

"Yeah, but she won't believe that."

"I'm sorry. She's your best friend."

"I look at it this way. If she keeps doing what she's doing, then, we aren't going to be best friends for long. She'll go off to Kitty-land, and I'll try to ride the sanity highway. So, if the goodbye comes a little early, well, that's just how it is."

"When did you get so old and wise?"

Cori shook her head. "I don't know. I think it was because Dad always said that he couldn't control what other people thought or did. He could only control himself. If people liked him, great. If they didn't like him, fine. He couldn't change that, so why try?"

Hope put an arm around Cori and pulled her close. "You still have to try and help her. You know that."

"I will, Mom. I'll try. You're going to help her too, right?"

"I'll do what I can."

Cori's phone pinged, and she pulled it out.

"Something important?" Hope asked.

"Yes and no. It appears the clamp down has begun."

Back in the house, Hope went to her office. She didn't feel all that good about what had happened. Adele's quick response bothered Hope. She thought that Adele would wait till Rob returned. They could formulate an action plan together, because they would both need to be on the same page. Lottie would exploit any chinks in their approach.

"Good evening, Mrs. Herring. How was your dinner?"

"Very good, Max. How was your day of hunting?"

Max still wore his tuxedo, and he looked ready for the queen's ball.

"Not fruitful, as far as the case is concerned. Yet, I don't think I misspent my time. I learned a great many things from the net."

"Nothing wrong with that. I have a question. In your day, when someone started hanging around with an unsavory character, what did you do?"

"Well, if the someone was dear to me, I would try and keep the two apart. If that was impossible, I tried reason, although reason rarely beat emotion. When all else failed, I would move on. When a ship is sinking, you don't swim into the whirlpool."

"Exactly. Then everyone drowns, right?"

"That was my experience. I will leave you to your email. Have a good night."

Max disappeared. Hope pulled up her email and sifted through the entries. The most intriguing email came from Jim Warren Sr. He wanted to know if she preferred Friday or Saturday night for their little date. Hope didn't know how to answer, as it seemed he had boxed her into one night or the other.

She chose Saturday.

# 19

By the time Saturday rolled around, Cori was in a funk and Hope wasn't in a good mood either. According to Cori, Lottie had ballooned into hurricane mode. While she was obeying, somewhat, she was not doing it willingly. Her rebellion had caused her to be "grounded," a term that had never been used in the Wells household. While Cori could chat with Lottie via computer for fifteen minutes a day, the two girls could not be together.

"I'm not Exotic Kitty," Cori complained. "Why can't she talk to me?"

"For the same reason you don't say 'no more spinach,' when your child doesn't eat dinner."

Cori chuckled. "Yeah, I get it. You have to cut off something people actually like."

Hope sipped coffee in the kitchen, having returned from her morning stint at the bakery. Her arms ached from the work, and she wondered if she could skip her "date" with Jim Sr. She could plead exhaustion or some other malady. That would be true, but it would probably nix any chance of getting him to make some sort of mistake and admit he killed his wife. If he were smart, he would call off the meeting. Hope didn't expect him to do that.

"Hey," Hope said, "how would you like to go with me to Jim Warrens' house?"

Cori made a face. "Why would I want to do that?"

"Because, I could use your company on the visit."

"You mean because he's sort of strange? I mean, he never stops smiling. He's weird. What person never stops smiling?"

"Apparently, Jim Warren Sr. Will you come?"

Cori grinned. "I get to be the chaperone?"

"Sure. And, you get to see if he really killed his wife."

"Did he do it?"

"He's a suspect."

"Then I'll be your bodyguard, too."

"Exactly. So what do you say? Come along with me?"

"I'm up for it. Do I have to wear something special?"

"Nope."

"Roger that."

~

The Warren house occupied a large lot in a golf community just outside Castle Park. Unlike the golf courses in her home state of Ohio, Pine Ridge was still green and filled with golfers.

"Seems odd, doesn't it," Cori said.

"What does?"

"People playing golf in November. Courses are beginning to close up North."

"The advantages of living in the South."

"Why don't you play golf?"

"I never had the chance. I wasn't one of the girls who belonged to the country club."

"Me, either."

They both chuckled as Hope pulled into the drive.

"Nice house," Cori said.

"All the houses in this place are nice. Now, he's not expecting you, so just go with the flow, okay?"

"Roger that."

Jim Sr.'s eyes narrowed when he spotted Cori, but his smile didn't fade. Hope knew that a man like him wouldn't be fazed by a young girl.

"Come in, come in," he said. "What a pleasant addition to our little party. You must be Cori."

"Pleased to meet you," Cori said and shook hands, which made Jim Sr. chuckle.

"My pleasure," he said. "How about a Coke?"

"Sure."

Jim left them in the Florida room, a large room with huge windows that made for lots of light. The green tile floor and large plants in the corners gave the room a jungle feel. The view was of the golf course, of a green with a pond in front. In the fading light, the scene was serene.

"Looks pretty," Cori said.

"Now, you know why Jim Warren Jr. is a golf pro."

"Yeah, I figured that. Just step out the back door and play."

Jim Sr. returned with a small tray that held a glass of red wine, a Coke, and a tumbler of what looked like whiskey. Hope accepted the wine, and Cori took the soda.

"Hey," Jim Sr. said to Cori, "how would you like

to see the basement game room. I believe there's a pinball machine that you might enjoy."

Cori gave her mother a hopeful look.

"Sure," Hope said. "Have at it." She watched her daughter disappear. So much for the bodyguard. In minutes, Jim Sr. was back, tumbler in hand.

"Nice view," Hope said.

"Seventh green," he said. "One of my favorite holes. How's the wine?"

"Good. Now, as I recall, I'm here to go over your list of possible suspects."

"Right, right, have a seat. Let's take a minute to relax before we get to business."

He sat on the couch, and she knew he expected her to join him. She was not so direct and took a chair across from the man. He grinned, a knowing grin. She suspected that he considered this some kind of game. She had met his first move with her own.

"Tell me," Hope said, "are you going to be able to stay here without Ardis?"

"I think so. She carried a fair amount of insurance, and that will keep me here."

"I guess I should clear up a point or two. Did you know Ardis was going to divorce you?"

For the first time, his smile slipped. She couldn't

tell if he was surprised by the information, or by the fact that she knew it.

"I won't lie to you," he said slowly. "I was aware that she was unhappy. But I didn't think she had reached that stage. Who told you she had plans to divorce me?"

"Her sister."

"Ah, yes, that makes sense. Abby is probably lying, as that's all she can do. She's lived on lies ever since I married her sister."

"She *might* be lying. I'm sure the police will check. I sent her to Detective Robinson."

Jim's mouth twitched. He was not enjoying this.

"I suppose he'll find out that she had hired a lawyer. I knew that.'

"Which gives you a reason to strike before the marriage was ended."

"You would think that, wouldn't you. I have to admit that it makes me look bad. But, I'll repeat what I told you before. I did not kill Ardis."

"I believe you. But, if you didn't, who did?"

He rubbed his face a moment. "If money is motive, then I would put Jim Jr. and Abby at the top of the list. They both need money desperately. I do too but not as desperately as them."

"And if money is not the motive?"

"Then, I would offer the vice principal. She was bitter because Ardis leapfrogged her and got the principal job. That would be motive enough."

"Were there any threats involved?"

"In the beginning, but they stopped. I don't know if that indicated a change of heart or was just some ruse to put Ardis off balance."

"What do you think?"

"I'm really not in a position to pass judgment. I mean, if you're going to look at people who disliked my wife, then you'll have to include the Penders. They went off the deep end when their daughter broke her neck."

"That was about five years ago, wasn't it?"

"It was, and they certainly calmed down after some time passed. I throw them out there because they were very nasty for a while."

"All right, I'll name the suspects. The Penders, Abby, Jim Jr., the vice principal, and ... you."

He nodded. "I'm afraid the husband is always a suspect."

"So, who did it?"

He looked across the room, thinking. "The method of death suggests someone with a bit of strength. I mean, Ardis was not a heavy woman, but if she was knocked out, she would be too much for a weak person."

"Are any of the suspects too weak?"

"I'm not sure. The vice principal and Abby are women, and I would think weaker than Jim Jr., Walter Pender, or me. So, I suppose, I would name Jim Jr. or Walter as the likely killer."

"That makes some sense. I know neither you nor your son have any sort of alibi, but what about Walter?"

"You'll have to talk to the police about that. I'm guessing he was somewhere at the gala in the school gym."

"He and his wife were Tweedledum and Tweedledee, weren't they?"

"Yes, and those were the best costumes in the gym. I was astounded. They looked exactly alike."

Hope sipped her wine. "Who were you with?"

He blinked more than once. "What?"

"When Ardis was killed, who were you with?"

"No one."

"I know there is a certain code that says you don't want to damage someone's reputation, especially when they're married. But, right now, you're number one on the suspect list."

"I hardly think—"

*Murder and Deception*

"Take a look around, Jimmy. You're living large here, and it was about to be taken away from you. As soon as Ardis filed for divorce, you would be out of here. I'm guessing you don't want to lower your standard of living."

He stared at Hope. "You're fishing."

"Not for long. The police will start getting names and following up. They'll find her."

"It's not what you think. Our relationship is purely platonic."

"I don't care. If she's your alibi, and she wasn't in on the killing, then, you're both off the hook. The police won't need to bring up her name at all."

"You make it sound as if they can keep her name out of the papers. We both know better. Sooner or later, people will know. In Castle Park, that means some rather dirty comments."

"It would be better for you to be upfront about this. If you were with someone, it will go better for you to name the person."

"Her name is Elaine Mathis."

"She's a teacher. I know her."

"Yes, well, she's having a rough go of things with her husband. She needed someone to talk to, and she didn't want to confide in Ardis."

"But she didn't mind confiding in you?"

"What can I say? Women trust me. I keep my mouth shut."

"Tell me, do you always go after married women?"

He smiled, and it was a sly smile, not the innocent one he usually used. "Why would you ask that?"

"Because, married women have a fallback position. If things don't work out with you, and they never do, then they can go back to their husbands ... provided you've been discreet."

"I'm always discreet."

"That's good, because there's always the risk of the husband finding out and coming for you."

"I'm very, very discreet."

"Thank you. The police will interview Elaine. If I have any say in the matter, I'll have them do it outside the station and the school. If she happens to run into Detective Robinson in my house, well, that's understandable. I work with the police all the time."

"Why would you do this for me?"

"Not for you. I don't care much about your reputation. I'm doing this for Ardis. If you didn't kill her, then I have to move on to the other suspects. And, I don't want Elaine to pay dearly for a simple mistake."

"She is a lovely woman. Wait, wait, now I understand. You're not doing this just for Ardis. You're a suspect. too. You found her in the car."

"Yes, I'm a suspect, too, but not a good one, since I don't have a motive. So, I would like very much to find the real killer."

"That's reassuring. I can't tell you how much I appreciate this. I'm sure Elaine will be happy as well."

"One more thing," Hope said. "From now on, I suggest you and Elaine cool it."

He stared at her a moment. "Ah ... do you want to take her place?"

"Not for all the tea in China. But, thanks for asking."

"Should you change your mind..."

"I won't. Don't call or text or email Elaine. I'll handle that. Thanks for the wine."

"You can't leave yet. You just got here."

"Sorry, Jimmy, this interview is over."

Hope and Cori left the house and drove out of the golf community to head for home. "Pizza?"

"I was winning," Cori said. "Another ten minutes, and I would have set a record."

"Knowing Mr. Warren, I would say that the game is set up to let newcomers win."

"You can do that in pinball?"

"You can cheat in any sort of game."

"Can I ask Lottie to come with us for pizza?"

"Lottie's grounded, isn't she?"

"Yeah, but I thought you might spring her for pizza."

Hope thought a moment before she answered. "All right. I'll make the call, on one condition. Lottie can't go to the restroom and change her outfit, and she can't use her phone."

"That's two conditions."

"Do you want her to come or not?"

Cori chuckled. "Two is fine."

## 20

The Pizza Corner wasn't busy, which was fine with Hope. She, Cori, and Lottie occupied a booth that afforded a view of the parking lot. It wasn't the best view, but it wasn't the worst either. To Hope, Lottie looked like a junkie in need of a fix. She was fidgety, running her fingers through her hair constantly, and her eyes darted back and forth. Lottie wanted something badly, and it showed.

"Since I have you here," Hope said to Lottie, "I'm going to pry a little."

"Mom," Cori said.

"We need to talk. Since Lottie spends so much time with us, I think it's a good idea to learn a little more about Exotic Kitty."

At the name, Lottie's eyes widened, as if she was surprised.

"As you might guess," Hope continued, "I don't know anything about Instagram or Exotic Kitty, so I'm asking you for some information. What can you tell me?"

Lottie looked away and squirmed. Hope waited, as silence was generally a good tactic.

"There isn't much to tell," Lottie said. "I mean, she's just someone I talk to online. She gives me ideas ... about ... things."

"Like what to wear and how to look?"

"Yeah. I need to use the restroom."

"Fine," Hope said. "Leave your phone on the table."

Lottie gaped, not sure she heard correctly.

"If you can't leave your phone, I'll take you home right now."

Lottie pulled out her phone and placed it on the table. Without a word, she slid out of the booth and headed for the restroom.

"Did you have to do that?" Cori asked when Lottie was out of earshot.

"I think so," Hope said. "I don't expect Lottie to tell us much. She's become used to lying, and that will continue. But, it's good to let her know that she's not fooling people."

"You don't think that she'll become even more secretive?"

"That's a risk, but you have to remember that she has limited resources. She can't drive. I don't think her allowance will get her far. And her internet access can be cut off in an instant."

"I don't think she's thought that far ahead."

"I know. People rarely thoroughly evaluate their position. Just how secure are they? Most of us forget that we rely on shaky networks."

"Like what?"

"Food and energy, for example. When you think about it, you have to figure out that there are a lot of steps from the farm to your plate. A severe interruption and you're scavenging for food."

"Yuck."

"The energy grid works the same way. Take out a generating plant or distribution station, and everything goes dark and cold."

"It's not cold in Castle Park."

"It can be cold in the winter," Hope reminded her daughter.

"You make it sound like we're barely hanging on."

"Look into how people lived a hundred years ago, when electricity wasn't so extensive. You'll be thanking your lucky stars that you're living now."

"I know, I know, can we talk about something else?"

Lottie returned from the restroom, and she looked calmer than when she had left. Hope wondered if Lottie had somehow managed to connect to the Internet. Not that it mattered.

"So. Exotic Kitty," Lottie said. "She's not that important ... not really. She just sort of gave me the courage to be myself."

"That's good," Hope said. "Where does she live?"

"Florida."

"How old is she?"

"Twenty-something."

"Family?"

Lottie shrugged.

"Sounds about right. All right, enough of the twenty questions." Hope pushed the phone back to Lottie. "Show me Exotic Kitty."

Lottie stared a moment and then smiled. "Sure, sure." She picked up the phone and started tapping the screen. Her thumbs moved too fast for Hope to follow. In seconds, she had an image on the screen, which she showed to Hope.

"Here she is. Exotic Kitty."

Hope looked at a picture of a young woman maybe in her twenties, with strange, tiger-striped makeup, a fluffed wig of blond hair, wearing a tiger striped bikini that didn't hide a lot. Her skin was bedecked with tattoos, mostly of cats—lions, tigers, black cats. There was a lot of jewelry around her neck and on her fingers and ears. Hope had the idea that the woman was a mixed metaphor of cats and bling.

"She's ... something," Hope said.

"She's not always like this," Lottie said. "I mean, she has lots of costumes and stuff. She knows a lot about makeup."

"I can tell. All right, that's enough. Let's forget about her for the time being."

The pizza arrived, and Hope doled out the slices to the girls.

"Don't eat too much," Hope said. "Save room for ice cream."

"Roger that," Cori said.

The longer Lottie was with Cori, the better she became. Hope didn't know if it was Cori's influence or the lack of Exotic Kitty input, but she wished that Lottie would come to realize that she didn't have to be in constant communication with the online presence.

"That was good. The food was great and Lottie acted more like herself," Cori said, after they had dropped off her friend.

"It was," Hope agreed. "But it won't last."

"Yeah, I know."

At home, Hope went to her office. Max had changed out of his tuxedo and into a bright red jogging suit.

"This is incredibly comfortable," Max said.

"I thought ghosts were always comfortable," Hope answered.

"We are ... mostly. We forget what it was like when we were alive. I'm relearning. My era could have benefited from such clothes."

"Agreed. Back to your searches. Have you had a chance to look into Doug's case?"

"A little. I've been so involved with the internet. Of course, I'll focus on the case soon, but I have this incredible urge to learn...everything. And, it's all out there. That's the part that is difficult to fathom. Everything is at my fingertips." He smiled and shrugged. "I apologize."

"I understand." Hope smiled at the ghost. "We all fight the distractions that keep us from things."

Cori's voice drifted into the office from the first floor. "Mom! Detective Robinson is here."

Hope nodded at Max, who faded away, then, she went downstairs. She found the detective in the kitchen where Cori had served him a cup of coffee from the Keurig machine.

"Derrick, how goes it?" Hope asked.

"It goes," he answered. "Your daughter is quite the hostess."

"Roger that," Cori said.

Derrick laughed. "And knows the lingo, too."

"Out you go," Hope told the teen and gave her a gentle push.

"Can't I listen? I might have some tips to hand over."

"Put them in writing," Hope said. "Or email them. That will help."

Cori rolled her eyes and left the room as Hope made herself a cup of coffee.

"Want something stronger than coffee?" she asked the detective.

"No thanks. I won't be here long. I just wanted to review the murder. I understand you have talked to all the Warrens, as well as the sister of the victim. Anyone else?"

"The vice principal also. She had a personal feud with Ardis."

"I talked to her, too. No alibi and a motive, but I'm not yet ready to make an arrest based solely on that."

"Do you think she's strong enough to have put Ardis into the car?"

"I think so. People are capable of more than they think, especially if stressed."

"Well, then, I haven't been able to eliminate anyone except Jim Warren Sr. He was doing some hanky-panky with Elaine Mathis, a teacher. I haven't talked to her. I'll leave that to you."

"I'll speak to her. But you don't think he's lying?"

"No, he lied when he said he was alone. Elaine is married. I don't think she's going to alibi him, unless it's true. And, if you can manage to keep the tryst out of the news, that would be appreciated."

"We can do that, provided she cooperates. So, that leaves the son, the sister, and the vice principal, right," Derrick said.

"Yes, but I haven't talked to the Penders."

"I have. I knew they had been very bitter when their daughter had the accident. But, they seemed to mellow a little over the years. Besides, they have a pretty solid alibi."

"They were with each other? That's hardly an alibi."

"No, he was in the restroom, and I have verified that. She said she was in the hall, although no one remembers seeing her. That sounds suspicious until you remember that she's physically disabled. She can't lift anything over twenty pounds. It's some sort of neurological disease. I verified that with her doctors. So, she wouldn't have been able to lift Ardis into the car."

"In that case, we're reduced to three suspects ... unless we've overlooked someone." Hope stared at her coffee mug, thinking.

"I don't know who. Ardis didn't have that many enemies."

"There's always that person who got slighted in high school, who never got over it."

Derrick laughed. "That's a good reason to move away from home. Hopefully that high schooler won't be able to find you."

"I hear you. Tell me, does the police department have any sort of cyber-crime team?"

"What are you thinking about? ID theft? Nigerian prince scams?"

"Cori's best friend is involved with a woman who goes by the screen name Exotic Kitty. This woman has a hold on Lottie Wells, and I was wondering if there was any legal recourse."

"We don't have anyone here, but the state police have a section. How about I refer this to them. They can take a look at this Exotic Kitty person."

"Great. Thanks. And, I'll see if I can help eliminate any of the remaining suspects in Ardis's murder."

"Roger that."

Hope laughed.

~

Monday found Hope at her desk, waiting for the day to begin.

"Good morning, Mrs. Herring."

"Good morning, Danielle."

Hope watched the girl head to her seat, and she couldn't help but wonder why Danielle came so early. Most of her students chatted in the hall until the last minute. Why get to class early?

"Danielle, can I ask you a question?"

"Sure."

"Why do you come in so early? I mean, why don't you hang out in the hall?"

"I don't have a smart phone. If you can't talk

about the net, people ignore you. Half the time, they text each other from four feet away. It's stupid."

"I see. Pretty strange, huh?"

"I know kids who go to the restroom and hide in the stalls so they can use their phones. It's weird."

"I happen to agree with you. Does anyone you know consider it all a big waste of time?"

Danielle shook her head. "You know how they talk about herd immunity for viruses and stuff? Well, they got part of it right. We're one big herd. One of these days, we're going to be led over a cliff or something."

"You have something there. I take it you don't subscribe to what the crowd thinks."

"Not if it's something stupid."

"Keep up the good work."

Danielle grinned.

At the end of the day, Hope took a few moments to think about the murder of Ardis Warren. Of the three remaining suspects, she didn't have a strong feeling about any of them. While they were all capable and in the vicinity when the murder occurred, they didn't seem all that dangerous.

With the exception of Abby maybe.

Hope had seen Abby's desperation firsthand. She lived in fear, and she needed money. Since Ardis was no longer going to give support, Abby was almost forced into doing something. That something could have been murder, disguised as suicide. Hope didn't think Abby was smart enough to know that the coroner would figure out how Ardis died. The suicide ruse was bound to come to light. What then? Abby didn't seem to have a part B to her plan. Yet, Hope had no real evidence. No one had seen Abby around the car or even at the gala. How was Hope going to prove anything?

Packing up, Hope headed for her car. She had just reached the parking lot when her phone pinged. She checked the message and saw it was from Cori.

*LOTTIE IS GONE!!!!!!*

## 21

All right," Hope said, as soon as Cori was safely strapped in her seat. "What do you mean Lottie is gone?"

"She left right after lunch." Cori spoke fast. "I didn't see her leave, so she has a head start."

"Her mother knows?"

"I called her. She was going to call the police."

"Tell me what happened."

"I thought Lottie was a lot better. She was really happy at school, even though she didn't change her clothes or anything. Right after lunch, she told me it didn't matter anymore. She was going to start a new life. That's how she put it ... a new life."

"You don't know what that means?"

"Nope." Cori was trying to keep from falling apart. "I asked her, but she said she'd tell me later."

"You didn't see her leave school?"

"No. After lunch, we go to different classes. It wasn't till after school that I figured out that she had left."

"She didn't ask you to keep her disappearance quiet?"

"No, she didn't say a thing about leaving or keeping it quiet."

"Well, I don't think we can do anything now. The police will probably issue an Amber alert. People will be looking for her."

"She did say something a little odd. She said she wouldn't be texting Exotic Kitty anymore and laughed like that was really funny."

Hope thought a moment. "Maybe because she was planning to go live with Exotic Kitty. No need to text when you're side by side."

"Oh, gosh, Mom. I didn't think of that."

"Get online and find out all you can about Exotic Kitty."

"You think Lottie went to her?"

"If you were Lottie, where would you go to start a new life?"

"Yeah, yeah, okay."

Hope drove fast, letting Cori concentrate on her phone. Where was Exotic Kitty? And, how was Lottie going to get to her?

As soon as Hope reached home, she hurried up to her office and Cori went straight to her laptop.

"Max," Hope called to the ghost since she didn't spot him at the computer.

"Yes, Mrs. Herring?" Max appeared by the door.

"You're not online?"

"I am taking a break. The lure of the internet must be resisted at times."

"I agree, but I need you right now. Do you think you can discover where Exotic Kitty lives?"

"I don't know. My internet skills are limited."

"You've spent a great deal of time online, so see if you can find her."

"I take it, Cori's friend has run away?"

"I think so, and I think she's headed for Exotic Kitty, wherever she is. Can you help us?"

"Certainly, Mrs. Herring. I will do whatever I can."

"Thanks, Max, thanks a lot. I'll check back with you in a bit. I need to talk to Adele and the police ... if I can."

Hope fixed herself a cup of coffee while she tried reaching out to Adele. The text from her was not encouraging, as there was no news of Lottie's whereabouts. Detective Robinson wasn't available, which put Hope in a stew. There was no information. As she sipped the coffee, she tried to think of any clues Lottie might have let slip out, anything that would help pinpoint the location of Exotic Kitty. Hope was convinced that Lottie was going to be with her idol.

"Any luck?" Hope asked Cori.

"No," Cori answered. "None of our friends know where Exotic Kitty lives. I can't find anything online that will help. I checked Amber Alerts, and there is one out for Lottie."

"Take a moment to go over what Lottie said today, word for word. Perhaps, there's a clue somewhere that will help."

Leaning on the table, Cori rested her chin in her hand. "I've done that, and I can't remember anything that will help."

"Nothing about someone picking her up? Nothing about a direction or state or city or anything?"

"No, the only part that now seems odd, although it didn't at the time, is that Lottie said she wouldn't have to duck into the bathroom stalls and change clothes anymore. I thought that she had decided to quit trying to be like Exotic Kitty, but I'm not sure that's what she meant."

"No, I think she meant she was leaving school and Castle Park. You know, I feel stupid for not seeing this coming." Hope paced around the kitchen.

"You feel stupid? Mom, I talk to her every day, and I didn't see it coming. Why would she run away?"

"She didn't run away, she ran toward something she thought was better. People do that sometimes. The grass is always greener on the other side of the fence."

"But, it's not, is it?"

"Not often. Keep looking. I'm going to my office, and I'll try to talk to the police. Maybe, they have something."

Max was busy on the computer when Hope entered. He had turned on the speakers and was listening as he surfed.

"Anything?" she asked.

"Not yet," he replied. "I'm going back in time, trying to find the first appearance of Exotic Kitty. There might be something there."

Hope's phone chirped, and she answered immediately. "Detective Robinson. What's the news?"

"Well, I'll start with Ardis Warren, as that's the easiest. No movement there, no arrests. On the Lottie Wells disappearance, I can tell you this, as it will soon be on the news. She left the school after lunch and was picked up by a white van. School security cameras picked it up, but not much else. There were no identifying elements on the grainy recording and no license plate. The driver wore a baseball cap and sunglasses, from what we can tell. Could be male or female."

"And, there are only about a zillion white vans in America."

"Exactly. It could have come from anywhere."

"Not very helpful."

"Not helpful at all, really. The tech guys are trying to enhance the footage. They might find something."

"All right. Thank you."

"One more thing. There was a short gap where Lottie was unaccounted for. After lunch and before pickup. She wasn't in class. We think she was hiding in a bathroom stall and texting the person in the van."

"That makes sense. She didn't want to be caught in the hall."

"I'll keep you informed. You do the same?"

"If Cori remembers anything helpful, I'll let you know."

After Hope ended the call, Max held up one hand.

"I might have something," he said.

"You do? What is it?"

"Well, it's not Exotic Kitty, it's Boo-Hoo Kitty. Different name, but I think there are similarities between them."

"Boo-Hoo Kitty?" Hope walked over to the desk and looked over Max's shoulder.

"The entries are several years old. The woman lacks the style and sophistication of her newer version. Boo-Hoo might have been some sort of trial run."

"Why do you say that?"

"Listen." Max turned up the speakers

Hope heard the voice of Boo-Hoo Kitty describe how to fake a tattoo.

"That's not a woman," Hope said. "That's a man faking a woman's voice."

"Exactly," Max said.

"So, we're looking for a man?"

"I would say so, if Boo-Hoo became Exotic."

"Have any idea where Boo-Hoo lives?"

"That's rather fortunate. It appears he lives in Castle Hayne."

"Right down the road?"

"Yes. He gave out his address in one of the videos, some sort of request for money. Rather tawdry, if you ask me."

"Max, you're a genius. I'd hug you if you were solid."

"It's probably nothing, Mrs. Herring. It's all conjecture."

"Never mind. Keep at it."

"Where are you going?"

"To pay a visit to Boo-Hoo Kitty."

Cori locked her seatbelt. "You think this is a good idea?"

"Yes and no," Hope said. "On one hand, this is most likely a wild goose chase. I mean, it's a leap from Boo-Hoo Kitty to Exotic Kitty, too big a leap to have the police involved yet. But, it's something, and it's close by, so you and I can be proactive. We'll drive by the address. If we spot a white van, we'll call the police."

"And if we don't spot a white van?"

"We'll knock on the door."

"And do what?"

"Sell Girl Scout Cookies."

"That's crazy. I'm no Girl Scout."

"You are now. You don't have the cookies. You're just taking orders."

"Mom, you can't just make up this stuff on the fly."

"Of course, we can. We check out the house and whoever answers the door. If we don't like what we see, we'll call the police. Otherwise, we'll spend an hour or two driving around the county looking for white vans."

"Why?"

"Because Lottie was picked up at school by a white van."

"Crapola."

"Exactly," Hope replied.

"I've never heard of Boo-Hoo Kitty."

"Not many people have. She's old news."

"Yeah, you know, I like this. We're detectives. Even if we're wrong, it will be kind of fun."

"I hope so."

GPS led Hope to an older, ranch-style house set off a county road. She guessed it had been a farm at one time, from the look of the several low, dilapidated buildings set away from the house.

"What are those?" Cori asked looking off in the distance.

"Hogs or turkeys," Hope said. "There are a lot of animal farmers around here."

"Yuck."

"Say that next Thanksgiving. Where did you think turkey and pork came from?"

"Not here."

"Without farms, we'd starve."

"We could raise our own food."

"And spend all day, every day doing it. Just be thankful."

"Roger that."

The early November sky was turning dark as Hope and Cori approached the house. Hope noted that the bushes needed trimming and the trees pruning. Most of the leaves were still on the trees which didn't surprise her. In North Carolina, autumn sometimes came late. The pine trees rose tall and straight. She didn't see a single light on inside the house. They parked and walked up the driveway.

"Remember, you're taking orders," Hope said.

Cori held up her phone. "Got it right here."

Hope stopped a few feet from the door, letting Cori walk up and knock. She thought they looked like what they were, a mother hovering over her young daughter.

"Don't go inside," Hope said. "Not for anything."

"Don't worry. I know what I'm doing, Mom."

Cori had to knock a second time before the door opened.

"Yes?" the man asked.

"Sorry to bother you," Cori said, "but I'm selling Girl Scout Cookies. I was wondering if you wanted to order some."

Hope studied the man in the doorway. To her, he looked at least sixty, mostly bald, with wispy, long white hair covering his ears. Blue T-shirt, faded jeans, slippers, he didn't look in particularly good shape. He smiled at Cori, which meant absolutely ... nothing.

"You're a little late, aren't you?" he asked. "I thought cookies were a spring thing."

"They are," Cori said. "I'm actually early. We're taking early orders this year. You look like a Thin Mint person to me."

"Come in, come in, let me get my wallet."

"I'm just taking orders," Cori said. "I'll collect the money when I deliver the cookies."

"Yeah, I remember how it goes. You got a brochure or something?"

Hope stepped forward, holding out her phone. "Here's a list of what's available."

"You must be her mother. You two look alike. Come on in, while I make up my mind."

His smile seemed genuine, but something about him made Hope uneasy. "We don't do that ... Girl Scout rules. We're not allowed to go into anyone's home," she said. "And, anyway, we don't want to put anyone out."

"Suit yourselves." The man took Hope's phone.

Cori moved to the side and looked past him, and he leaned against the door jamb to block her view. She stepped back, as if anxious.

"Gotta pee?" he asked.

"Just tired," Cori said. "We've been at this for a while."

"I imagine. Well, you're right, young lady, I am a Thin Mint fan. I'll take four boxes."

"Terrific. Name?" Cori pretended to put his information into her phone app.

"Walt, Walter Mitty."

As he rattled off the address, he handed back Hope's phone. She noted the tattoo on his forearm, a black cat. She remembered that Exotic Kitty had several tattoos, including black cats. Coincidence?

"Thank you so much," Cori said. "As soon as the cookies get here, I'll deliver them."

"I'll be looking forward to it."

"Thank you," Hope said. "My daughter is trying to earn enough points for a vacation at Disney World."

"Now, I can appreciate that. I was there once. Have a good evening."

Hope and Cori turned for the car.

"Look back and wave," Hope whispered.

Cori half turned and waved to the man who waved back. "Why did you want me to do that?" she asked, as she slid into the car.

Hope noted that the front door had closed, and the man was back inside.

"Because, if he's a bad person and he went for a gun or something, we needed to know."

Cori shook her head. "You're more paranoid than I am."

"Situational awareness, Cori, stay alert. What did you think of him?"

"He's weird, but he doesn't look like Exotic Kitty."

"Did you notice the tattoo?"

"Yeah, a black cat."

"That's one strike. Number two is that he lied about his name."

"Walter Mitty?"

"It's the title of a short story about a man who has fantastic daydreams. In reality, he's a henpecked husband."

Cori stared back at the house as Hope started the engine and began to pull away from the curb.

"What now?" Cori asked.

"Well, giving a false name isn't a crime, but that doesn't really matter." Hope handed her phone to Cori. "Dial Detective Robinson."

When Cori started to dial, Hope pulled to the side of the road. She could no longer see the house, but she could see the driveway to the house. That was good enough.

"It's ringing." Cori handed back the phone.

Hope spent the next few minutes convincing the detective that he needed to come out and roust the man in the house. It sounded like a dead end, but Hope managed to wheedle a promise out of the detective. That was good enough.

She ended the call and stared down the road.

"How long are we going to do this?" Cori asked.

"Until the police get here."

"That could be hours?"

"Don't you have homework?"

"I didn't bring my backpack."

"I'll explain to your teachers."

"I doubt they'll understand."

"Oh, I think they will."

"Why is that?"

"Because there's a white van coming out of the driveway from that house."

"No way." Cori's head spun to look down the road.

"Call Detective Robinson again."

"Roger that."

## 22

Hope fell in behind the white van, praying that the driver wouldn't spot her. But she knew better. If the man had Lottie in the van, he might be more than a little suspicious. He would be checking his mirrors constantly.

The only advantage she had was that the daylight was fading fast. It would be more difficult to spot her in the dark. Of course, that worked both ways. She would have to try and keep cars from getting in between them. That wouldn't be easy. Had the man noted her SUV when she pulled away? She guessed he had. After all, she and Cori had spooked him, or so it seemed.

"Here." Cori handed over the phone. "It's Detective Robinson."

Hope spent the next several minutes telling the Detective about the man in the van and that they were following him.

"You shouldn't be doing that," Robinson warned.

"I know, but if he's making a break for it, finding him again will be very difficult. God knows what he'll do to Lottie." Hope gave the detective the license plate number.

"I'm going to alert the sheriff. I'll ask him to have a deputy join the parade. When the deputy pulls the van to the side of the road, keep going. There is no reason for you to hang around, all right?"

"You got it."

"Keep your phone handy. I'll call you back."

Hope squinted into the deepening dark.

"Are you going to turn on your lights?" Cori asked.

"In a minute. I want him to think I turned off, and some other vehicle pulled in behind him."

"He'll fall for that?"

"Probably not, but it's worth a try."

"You think Lottie's in the van?"

"I'm not sure. I think that man is up to no good since he took off right after we left. But, it could be as simple as him going off to work."

"He didn't look like he was going to work."

"I know, but looks can be deceiving. He didn't resemble Exotic Kitty either, did he?"

Cori laughed. "He wasn't even close."

"Which is easy to do on the net. Lots of things online can be extreme. It can be the best or the worst of things."

"Like what?"

"Like a dating site. The pictures are usually the best one a person can post. Often, they are several years old because the person looked better when they were younger. Or, for resorts and vacation spots, the advertisers make everything look great, bigger, even the food. But, you know your food probably won't look like what they post on the internet."

"You're right. Hmm, I guess you can't trust what you see."

Hope flipped on her lights when she spotted the blue, blinking lights in her mirror. She pulled to the side to allow the sheriff's cruiser to pass. Slowing, she followed, as the cruiser pulled up to the van. When the van pulled over, the cruiser followed and stopped. Hope passed by, slowed, and pulled to the side.

"What are you doing?" Cori asked. "We're supposed to keep going."

"The deputy is probably alone. We're not going to get out, just watch."

"Why?"

"So the man in the van doesn't think he can do something to the deputy and run."

"I don't like this."

"I don't like it either, but it's what a good citizen does. And we're safe at this distance away from the van. I wouldn't put you at risk."

Hope turned in her seat to watch.

Behind her, the man from the farm stepped out of the van. With alarming speed, he shoved the deputy out of the way and ran ... straight for Hope's vehicle.

"Crap," Cori said. "Mom, drive!"

Hope watched the man approach, and she unlocked her door. At the last moment, she threw open the door, and the man couldn't stop to avoid it. He crashed into the SUV door and dropped to the ground.

That was enough for Hope. She put the car in gear and shot ahead another hundred yards. Then, she stopped. Looking back, she saw the deputy handcuff the man.

"Get out with me," Hope told Cori.

"What? Why?"

"Lottie."

Hope led Cori back to the van while the deputy was busy putting the fleeing man into the cruiser. In seconds, Hope covered her hand with her sleeve and opened the rear door of the van. She didn't want to interfere with any prints left on the handle.

Peering inside, she saw the rolled carpet and what appeared to be a body inside.

"Oh, no." Hope moved her daughter back. "Cori, stay right here. Look away."

Climbing into the van, the officer managed to unroll the carpet enough to uncover Lottie, gagged and bound. "She's alive."

Cori spun around and looked into the van at her friend. "You're okay now. You're safe." The teen's voice was hoarse and a couple of tears rolled down her cheeks.

Hope told the officer, "Her name is Lottie Wells. She's the girl on the Amber Alert."

Two more sheriff cruisers pulled to a stop with lights flashing.

"We did it, Mom, we found her."

"We did." Hope hugged her daughter. "If you ever start changing clothes in the school bathroom stall, I'm going to ground you for life."

"Roger that."

It took another hour for Hope to sort out things with the deputies. During that time, Lottie was transferred to an ambulance which whisked her away to the waiting hospital.

Hope slowly drove back to Castle Park.

"Pizza?" Hope asked.

"Take out," Cori answered. "I have homework."

"I figured."

At home, Cori disappeared into her room with Bijou while Hope put the pizza in the oven to heat. She was no fan of cold pizza, although she had eaten her share in college. In those days, she did a lot of things she no longer found healthy.

It was while she poured milk that she thought about Lottie and how she managed to fool her mother for so long. Of course, Exotic Kitty had fooled Lottie, too.

Changing clothes in the bathroom stall.

Something about that bothered Hope. She couldn't lay her finger on it, but she needed to think more. Then, her phone chirped.

"Detective Robinson," Hope said. "All is well?"

"It is for Lottie," he said. "She's in the hospital for observation. Her captor gave her some drug, but she'll be all right. Luckily, you found her before he could do more harm."

"Lucky guess," Hope said.

"Yeah, lucky like a fox. You can give me all the details in the morning. I just wanted you to know that thanks to you and Cori, Lottie will be fine."

"Nightmares, Derrick, she'll have nightmares for a long while."

"She won't be the only one. While I have you, any ideas on the Ardis Warren case?"

"No, I'm stuck. Tell me again about the Penders. Where were they when Ardis was murdered?"

"Well, according to their testimony, he was in the restroom. He came in and went right into a stall, according to a man already in there. And, she said she was in the gym, although I haven't found anyone to confirm that."

"Because she wasn't there."

"What are you talking about?"

"Tweedledum and Tweedledee."

"What about them?"

"They're twins. They look exactly alike."

"You're saying..."

"I'm saying that *she* went into the restroom and hid in a stall. He went outside and killed Ardis. Of course, the man in the restroom would assume it was another man in the stall."

"Any way to confirm your theory?"

"Phones. Check their phone records and see if they were calling or texting before and after the murder."

"They're husband and wife. I would expect them to text."

"See if the text messages or email are still available. You might find out something."

"Good idea ... and thanks."

Hope smiled. What she had told the detective made sense. The couple had decided to dress up like twins. The Penders needed to confuse everyone. They also wanted to avenge their daughter.

After dinner, Hope trudged up to her office. Max was on the computer, reading away.

"Bravo, Mrs. Herring," Max said. "Your exploits are all over the net."

"Already?"

"I have surmised that many people pay attention to police communications."

"I suppose so. By the way, I think we've solved the murder of Ardis Warren."

"Indeed?"

"I think the Penders did it. He killed Ardis while his wife pretended to be him. Since they looked exactly the same in those costumes, no one noticed."

"A rather clever ruse."

"It sure was."

"Will the girl be all right?"

"Lottie went to the hospital, but I don't think she was injured. She's a lucky girl."

"Not lucky, just the friend of a very clever woman. I salute you."

"It was just some lucky guessing."

"I have found some details about your husband's accident, but they are all things that you already know. I am no closer to finding a solution, but it is early yet. I will continue the search."

"You'll get there, Max." Hope looked at her ghost. "And anyway, I'm glad you decided to stay here for a while."

"I'm in no hurry to leave. For the first time in a century, I feel a bit more content. There will be plenty of time to move on. There is no rush."

"In that case, hang around. Cori and I enjoy your company. It's like you're part of the family."

"It is very nice of you to say so. I will wish you a good night."

Max faded away, leaving Hope to work on her computer. Next to her on the desk was a vase of flowers that Luke had dropped off with a card that read: *To the best amateur detective in all of North Carolina.* A little heart was drawn on the card.

Looking at the colorful arrangement brought a smile to her face.

She'd decided she wasn't going to do much work, just email and a little grading. That would be enough. Even as she worked down the list, several congratulatory emails arrived in her inbox. The word was out. She had found Lottie Wells. Hope was getting famous.

At school the next day, the acting principal paid tribute to Hope during the morning announcements. Hope blushed while Elizabeth spoke in glowing terms of how she and Cori saved Lottie Wells. To hear her, it seemed Hope was a one-person detective agency.

She knew better. She and Cori had followed the clues. The kidnapper had panicked. It was that simple.

∽

After school, Derrick Robinson walked into Hope's classroom.

"You did it again," Derrick said.

"Did what?"

"Don't pretend you don't know. We found some texts between the Penders that were pretty graphic.

They didn't actually admit to murder, but it can be inferred. When we questioned them apart, Mr. Pender broke down. He had never been the leader in the household. Mrs. Pender told him what to do, and he did it. That included murder. He seemed almost relieved to be able to admit to the crime.

After Mrs. Pender heard about his confession, she confessed, too. She was happy that Ardis Warren had paid for her sins. You'll be happy to know that it went down as you said. Mrs. Pender sat in the stall while her husband did the dirty work."

"They probably thought that after all these years no one would suspect them."

"Mrs. Pender never forgot. And, the money ran out right after her daughter died. They were in financial trouble and had lost their daughter, while Ardis Warren was going places. It didn't seem right, or fair to them."

"It wasn't fair, but life often isn't fair." Hope's mind went to her husband's death for a moment. "Things can change in a heartbeat."

Derrick nodded. "The sheriff hasn't finished his investigation of the man you kept from running away. It appears that Lottie wasn't the first girl to run to him. His house contained a soundproof room in the basement, a kind of torture room. There are some blood stains. He's not talking, but he's in big, big trouble."

Hope groaned.

"He'll be in prison for a long time. You're a hero, Hope, as well as the best detective in America."

Hope laughed. "Hardly. If I were, I would have solved a certain case that seems quite simple on the surface."

Derrick nodded. He knew Hope had suspicions about the way her husband had died.

"It's a story from the past," she told him. "Maybe someday, I'll be able to tell you how it ends."

∽

Hope was stirring chicken soup on the stove, when Cori bounced in, all smiles, with Bijou running after her.

"I talked to Lottie." Cori picked up the cat and snuggled her while Bijou purred.

"How is she?"

"Great, well, not great, but better. I think she realizes how foolish she was about Exotic Kitty."

"Let that be a lesson. The internet is not to be believed."

"Don't I know it. Oh, and Lottie says thank you."

"Tell her she's welcome. Someday, she might have to return the favor."

"Roger that."

Cori pranced out of the kitchen with the cat chasing after her, and Hope smiled. Since Lottie was so young, it was probable that she would recover without many permanent scars. Time was a great healer.

In fact, time had caused Hope to forego unraveling the encrypted files her husband had left her. She felt a bit guilty about that. She needed to get back to that project, but the whole thing was so hard to face.

With a sigh, she decided to start again as soon as she finished dinner.

## 23

Hope sat at her desk and opened one of her husband's files.

*I once read about a writer who claimed he suffered from reverse paranoia. He was afraid that people were plotting to make him happy. That might be an enviable paranoia to have.*

*Unfortunately, paranoia doesn't come in flavors. It's a one-way street. You're scared that people are out to get you. Then, the problem becomes...what if you're right?*

*This story I'm researching has taken me all over the Midwest, especially in my home state of Ohio. I have interviewed people who remember quite well and people who can't remember much of anything.*

*The only common thread so far is whether or not the people worked for a nonexistent chemical company. Well, it's non-existent now, and the powerful have done their best to erase the company from history. That it ever existed is a toss-up. There are a few clues—not many— and they are not definitive. I believe, because I...believe.*

*And, it's not paranoia ... if it's true.*

*I have become a studier of shoes.*

*I know that doesn't make much sense, but it's a sure-fire way to determine if the same person is following you. While operatives can readily change coats and hats and glasses and fake mustaches, they rarely are able to swap shoes on a whim. It takes too much time, and if your job calls for staying on your feet for eight hours, you wear good shoes. I learned that from an aging detective who had spent more than a few years on the job.*

*Shoes. Who would have thought?*

*Now, if I think someone is following me, I check out his shoes. Other details are passed over and forgotten, but not shoes. Yesterday, the same shoes followed me around the mall. I'm pretty sure they were the same shoes. When the shoes are popular and common, you have to fall back to a second detail ... height for instance. Those people on your tail can't rise and fall like the tide. They're one height only.*

*Same shoes, same height, same person.*

*Cars are much trickier.*

*You see the same car over and over, when you're*

*looking for it. Same shape, same color, same model, same manufacturer. You pass it, and twenty miles farther, you pass it again. Can't be the same car, and yet, you wonder.*

*If you're being tailed by multiple cars, it's almost impossible to spot them. You have to keep driving, and that takes concentration. Trying to suss out vehicles that are after you makes for accidents.*

*I've given up on that. If they want to follow me, so be it.*

*Yeah, I guess I am paranoid. I'm being followed by people who don't have my best interests at heart. No, I'm not paranoid. I'm a victim, an enemy of someone or something.*

*I can only guess who, although I can guess why. I've learned too much about a certain company and a certain chemical. Worse, I'm a journalist. That makes me expendable.*

*What to do?*

*It seems silly to believe that my enemies will try to kill me. There's no reason for that. They'll discredit me first. That makes sense. Deny me employment, paint me as insane, siphon off all money and assets, create false stories to ruin my character and career. That would be more than enough.*

*Will they do those things? I'm pretty sure they're already trying. Being followed and probably videotaped, they might be able to edit and create a highlight reel that shows me killing someone. That would be damaging ... and more than enough to get me off the story.*

*I should probably delete this little essay. When they find it, and they will, they will point out how nuts I became at the end. Instead, I'm going to encrypt this and put it with the rest of the stories and essays I've written.*

*In time, with luck, and God willing, someone will read this and wonder.*

*Perhaps, that someone will take up the quest.*

*Someone will finish this story, because I'm afraid I will never get the chance.*


Hope stared at the computer screen.

Paranoia. She knew the feeling, although she had felt less and less scared the longer she lived in Castle Park.

"Mrs. Herring."

Hope turned to Max who wore a zoot suit from the 1940s. He looked like a criminal.

"Nice duds," Hope said with a grin.

"Thank you ... I think. I have a topic I wish to discuss with you."

"And, that is?"

"I think I might have found something."

I hope you enjoyed *Murder and Deception*! The next book in the series, *Deadly Mistakes*, can be found here:

viewbook.at/DeadlyMistakes

**THANK YOU FOR READING!**

Books by J.A. Whiting can be found here:
www.amazon.com/author/jawhiting

To hear about new books and book sales, please sign up for our mailing list at:
www.jawhiting.com

Your email will never be sold, shared, or spammed.

If you enjoyed the book, please consider leaving a review. A few words are all that's needed. It would be very much appreciated.

# BOOKS BY J. A. WHITING

SWEET COVE PARANORMAL COZY MYSTERIES

LIN COFFIN PARANORMAL COZY MYSTERIES

CLAIRE ROLLINS PARANORMAL COZY MYSTERIES

MURDER POSSE PARANORMAL COZY MYSTERIES

PAXTON PARK PARANORMAL COZY MYSTERIES

ELLA DANIELS WITCH COZY MYSTERIES

SEEING COLORS PARANORMAL COZY MYSTERIES

OLIVIA MILLER MYSTERIES (not cozy)

SWEET ROMANCES by JENA WINTER

COZY BOX SETS

**BOOKS BY J.A. WHITING & NELL MCCARTHY**

HOPE HERRING PARANORMAL COZY MYSTERIES

TIPPERARY CARRIAGE COMPANY COZY MYSTERIES

# BOOKS BY J.A. WHITING & ARIEL SLICK

## GOOD HARBOR WITCHES PARANORMAL COZY MYSTERIES

# BOOKS BY J.A. WHITING & AMANDA DIAMOND

## PEACHTREE POINT COZY MYSTERIES

## DIGGING UP SECRETS PARANORMAL COZY MYSTERIES

# BOOKS BY J.A. WHITING & MAY STENMARK

## MAGICAL SLEUTH PARANORMAL WOMEN'S FICTION COZY MYSTERIES

## HALF MOON PARANORMAL MYSTERIES

# VISIT US

www.jawhiting.com

www.bookbub.com/authors/j-a-whiting

www.amazon.com/author/jawhiting

www.facebook.com/jawhitingauthor

www.bingebooks.com/author/ja-whiting

J. A. WHITING BOOKS

Made in the USA
Monee, IL
21 October 2024